A SCENT OF NEW-MOWN HAY

A Scent of
New-Mown Hay

JOHN BLACKBURN

NEW ENGLISH LIBRARY
TIMES MIRROR

*NEL Books are published by New English Library Limited from Barnard's Inn,
Holborn, London, EC1N 2JR*
Made and printed in Great Britain by Love & Malcomson Ltd., Redhill, Surrey.

45003138 1

CHAPTER ONE

At the corner of the old cathedral building he turned right and began to walk up the long slope towards the station.

Very often he had taken this walk, and always at the same time of the evening ; tonight, however, he was late.

He was a small man and very neat. The thin cloth of his petty official's uniform was shiny with much pressing and his state-issue boots gleamed dully with inferior polish. A punctual and reliable man one would have thought. And this made it odd, because although he was late he did not appear to hurry.

As he went up the slope his usual precise gait seemed erratic and sloping. Sometimes his foot slurred off the pavement and trailed in the gutter. Twice he stumbled and leaned for a moment against the rusty iron railings. Passers-by noticed him, and grinned as they looked at his uncertain steps. But their conclusions were wrong. Although in the dim light of the badly lit city he might appear drunk, he had no alcohol in his stomach. All he had there was one large, soft nosed bullet. He was quite sober and he was dying.

As the man walked and staggered and died he gave thanks. He gave thanks to God, in whom he had no particular belief, for his starless night, and he thanked Comrade Radin, mayor of the city, for his inefficient lighting plant. Together they screened his way and hid from the eyes of the curious the thick, oily drops that fell behind him and mingled with the dust of the pavement.

On the station approach he prayed and reassured himself. 'Let it be easy,' he prayed, 'just this once let it be easy. Let them not be waiting for me at the barrier this time. Let the numbers be clear this time. Let it be easy. This is the last time you'll have to do it, the last time you'll ever have to do anything again. It must be all right this time because you can't stand much more, so just this once let it be easy.

'But you will be all right,' he told himself, 'they can't have followed you yet and you've such a little way to go, such a little way. That's right, up the stairs now, hold the rail and mind that woman with the baby, you mustn't bump into anybody now. Nearly there. You'll be in the booking hall in a moment. Keep to the dark side, away from the queues by the ticket office and the lights on the political posters. No guards at the barrier then. They're keeping the inspection for the frontier. An efficient and sometimes economical people.'

Slowly and haltingly, the man walked through the barrier and along the platform beside the train. He passed the coaches of the officers, the steaming dining car, and the crowded compartments of the shaven, blond soldiers who shouted and laughed at him as he stumbled by. He smiled foolishly at them and dragged himself on past the end of the passenger coaches to where the long line of baggage wagons stretched forward to the engine.

As he reached the trucks, the man's steps seemed to grow firmer. He no longer stared aimlessly at the ground but peered keenly at the doors of each truck and in particular at the white metal plaques that gave the details of their cargo and destination.

At the third door from the engine he halted. Very carefully he examined the plaque and then with a sigh leaned heavily against it. He raised his right hand, placed something between the gap formed by plaque and door and then remained motionless.

The four policemen and the dog came up the stairs at a run. For a time they had lost his trail, but in the street the dog had caught and followed the blood spoor. They paused for a moment in the hall and then ran through the barrier and along the train.

The man was waiting for them against the door. He moved very slightly as the sergeant reached him and then fell at his feet. He was quite dead.

After a time they cleared the waiting room and laid him on a bench beneath pictures of the country's leaders.

'No,' said the sergeant, 'no, there was only one and he's here. Yes, Comrade Station Master, the train can start on time. That's right, whenever you're ready, Comrade Station Master.'

For half an hour they left the man on his bench. His dead eyes were open and seemed to smile slightly at a photograph of the Minister of Rest and Culture.

Through the night the long train clattered and groaned towards the frontier.

*

Although London was at its hottest July, the office windows were tightly closed and an electric fire glowed in the grate.

The heat beat on the frosted glass partition of the secretary's cubicle and made life barely supportable to Miss Bond as she bent over the hundreds of reports before her, but to General Kirk, head of Her Majesty's foreign office intelligence service, it was a near approach to heaven.

Smiling like a contented cat, he put down the cigar with which he had been thickening the already overpowering atmosphere and lifted the ringing telephone beside him.

'Oh, it's you, Igor, how very nice. But of course, my dear chap, come up as soon as you like. What! From the army people you say, that's odd, they're usually so reluctant to part with any of the crumbs they sometimes manage to glean. And you and your boys can make nothing of it. Odder still. Right you are, come up at once.'

The man who entered the room a few minutes later was tall, stooping, and completely hairless. His dark suit was dandified and there was a bright flower in his buttonhole. His bored, vacant expression gave him the air of a well-bred rentier, but the air was false. He worked very hard for his living and he had been born in a Paris slum. He was Igor Trubenoff, head of the department dealing with Soviet Russia and at the moment a very puzzled man.

He gave a fine bow to Miss Bond as she opened the door to him, and preparing himself for martyrdom walked into the stifling room.

'My dear boy, come in and sit down.' The general's hand which lacked three fingers waved him to a seat.

'Have they got that wretched lift working yet? No! I've been on to them three times this morning and they don't seem to be doing a bloody thing. No fun working on the top floor these days. No fun at all. Now, my boy, tell me about it. What's the problem?'

'Well, sir, I just can't make it out. Either the army people are being hoaxed and they don't seem to think so, or something quite extraordinary is going on. See for yourself, sir.'

He took a thin slip of paper from his pocket and handed it to Kirk.

For a long time the General looked at the paper and his heavy, aristocratic features registered nothing at all. His multilated hand drummed quietly on the desk.

'Yes, yes, I see. They were quite right to let us have this, weren't they? Tell me, Igor, have you heard anything that might even remotely tie up with it? Anything at all?'

'No, sir, absolutely nothing.' His voice was everything the public schools and Oxford could make it, but it still remained strangely foreign. 'Since the last report I sent you things have been very quiet. It does seem as if this new policy of theirs is genuine.'

'I see. Then either somebody is playing a rather dubious joke on our friends in the army, or the Ruskis are up to something very big. Something that they're doing everything in their power to conceal.'

He heaved himself up from his chair and crossed the room to a small switchboard. There was a whirring sound and a map showing the Northern areas of European Russia spread itself across the wall.

'Now, Igor, where are we?'

Trubenoff pointed to two small, hardly noticeable dots on the vast area.

'Here we are, sir, Purflu, and here Karen.'

'Yes, quite a distance, isn't it. About three hundred thousand square miles at the outside. Quite an area. Now let's just go through this as if it was correct, which I doubt. Have you got any details of the agent yet?'

'No, sir, not yet,' said Trubenoff. 'They're having to send through to Berlin for the full particulars. They promised to let us have them as soon as they get them. All they know him by is a registered number X.10.'

'I see, well let's suppose for a moment that M'sieu X.10 has been telling the exact truth. What does he say?'

He moved ponderously back to the desk and looked at the paper.

'He says very little, doesn't he? Just a few notes, but then he had to be short because he was in a hurry. His use of plain language instead of code makes that clear. What did he want to say, that's the point?'

The Russian paused and put a cigarette to his lips and lit it with a thin gold lighter. His face seemed completely vacant as he looked at the map, inhaling deeply, and when he did speak his voice was very far away and dreamlike.

'An area of three hundred thousand square miles. An area between Purflu and Karen, a restricted area. One week ago they brought troops up from the south in thousands and completely encircled this area. They put a cordon from here to here.'

His finger traced a line on the cloth.

'They evacuated every living human being between these points and burnt tens of villages from one end to the other. The inhabitants have been put into camps surrounded by the most strict security precautions. The area is said to be expanding.'

'Yes,' said Kirk. 'Yes, I think that's significant. The area is said to be expanding. Ah, what is it, my dear?'

8

Miss Bond tripped into the room and put a small black folder on the desk.

'This was sent over from the War Office for Mr. Trubenoff, General,' she said, and went silently out.

The two men bent over the folder and opened it. It was the file on a man who had recently died.

There was a picture of him on the first page, and he was completely ageless. He stood against a wall, very smart in a marine officer's uniform, and he might have been any age. He might have been one of fifty nationalities, only his expression was typical. The ageless, nationless face had an expression of cynicism and at the same time of sentimentality. Of fanaticism and of the complete acceptance of evil. It was the face of central Europe.

The particulars below the picture had been written in indelible ink in a fine gothic hand. Trubenoff read them slowly.

'X.10, alias Paul Machieski, alias Gregor Hoffman, alias Kurt Arabin. Born Gdynia 1910, entered Polish Mercantile Marine nineteen—' He broke off and looked at Kirk.

'Entered Polish Mercantile Marine as cadet nineteen twenty-five,' he said very quietly and he was not reading from the file any more.

'Second officer on the Pilsudski when she entered allied waters. Relieved of his duties on applying for special service and was placed in the department of General, then Colonel Charles Kirk. Dropped three times over Poland and was intermediary agent at Peenemunde. Transferred War Office nineteen forty-six.'

He looked at the recent note at the bottom of the file and his voice was a whisper.

'Died Warsaw nineteen fifty-seven.'

'So, Paul is dead.' Kirk got up and crossed to the fire rubbing his hands before the glowing bars, and Trubenoff knew that his passion for heat was no luxury but a deep physical need.

'You know, Igor, we're old men now. We've sat in this dusty, unknown building that nobody normal ever comes to for a great many years.

'Every morning we pass the brass plaque bearing names of the office staff and every name is a lie. We sit in our rooms and lift telephones that are listed in no directory and people tell us things, and most of the things are unpleasant. Very soon, because we're old, they'll retire us, and when we do retire we'll have none of the satisfaction that other elderly retired gentlemen get. We'll have few old friends to talk to because we've sent most of our friends to their deaths. We won't talk about what we've done or write our reminiscences because we

9

won't be allowed to. But if we were allowed to we could tell some very nasty stories, and I have a feeling that this might be the worst of them all. Well, Igor, let's get on. Paul has done his job, let's do ours. What are they doing there? Just what are they up to?'

He straightened himself and moved to the map.

'Tell me about this area, Igor,' he said. 'This area that our friends have evacuated, burnt, surrounded with troops. I see points on a map. I see its size. I see that it is bordered by the Arctic. But what about it? How many people live there? Is there any industry or agriculture? What are its minerals, its commercial potentialities?'

'There is very little habitation, sir. The strip along the coast is tundra marsh and not cultivated at all. There are of course a few fishing villages but very few in size and number. The sea is frozen during the winter, and life is difficult. Further inland of course there is timber which is valuable. Most of the stuff they export from Archangel comes from there. You'll remember that new pulp plant they made such a fuss about last year. That is supplied from Karen. There must be a number of lumber camps dotted here and there but I don't suppose they employ many people. A few thousand at the most. There are no minerals worth exploiting.'

'Thank you, Igor!' He put a match to his cold cigar. 'That gives us a picture anyway. A picture of a bleak, sparsely populated area with no minerals and no great commercial value except for the timber. Except for the timber which gives it at least some significance. Well, what are they up to? Do they want it for a bomb range? I think not, they've got hundreds of other areas far more worthless than this, and whatever we may think about your countrymen, Igor, they are not spendthrifts. No, not a bomb range. Then what else? Some kind of minor political upheaval, a small revolt like they had in Georgia? I doubt it. I can't see a few fishermen and woodcutters putting them to such trouble. Not that then. What we must look for, I think, is something special to the area itself that is important. Something possibly about its position on the map. Something specific to it.'

He stared hard at the map for a moment and his hand played on the blue fringe that was the Arctic Ocean.

'Tell me, my boy,' he said after a while. 'Have you heard about what our American friends are rather picturesquely calling Operation Starbright?'

'Yes, a little, but only a little. I am afraid my technical education is sadly incomplete.'

10

'And mine, Igor, and mine. Still, from the little I do understand it might fit. Let's have old Mott in.'

Mrs. Mott was probably the most valuable piece of machinery in the building. There was no electronic brain that could rival her memory, no tabulating machine that could match her, for she was not human. She had no humanity in her, no warmth, no imagination, no creative urge. She was merely a record of forgotten facts, nothing else. It was hard to imagine there ever was a Mr. Mott, but there had been and he had died miserably in a Bayswater flatlet after ten years of matrimonial bliss. But for all this she was one of Kirk's greatest assets.

She sat stiffly before them and answered their questions and as she answered them they began to see at least a possible solution to their problem.

Now that the Americans had caught up with Russia, it seemed as if the day of the small world satellite was finished and both sides were working on something else. And this time it was the real thing. The thing which would give absolute power to its first inventors. A giant, manned, navigable structure in the sky which would return at will to any part of the Earth's surface.

They listened meekly to the flow of technicalities. The questions which had been answered. The enormous weights involved and the need for atomic thrust. Then the final, unsolved problem of deceleration and return which had brought the Americans to a standstill.

When she had left them they grinned shyly at each other and then Kirk got up and once more looked at the map.

'Well, do you think she's got anything?'

'I don't know, sir, it could be that. As she said, no one can calculate a course at that speed or distance, so if they were trying their first flight they would have to clear an area of about that size, and to make the journey shorter, they would put it near the poles.

'It could be that. There's the new plant they've got at Ittursk. It's huge apparently, but we haven't got an idea what they're doing there. Yes, it might be this satellite, sir.'

'Right, then let's leave it like this. What we know is, that for some reason the Russians have suddenly cleared a large area. We have no definite idea why they have done this, but it seems likely that it may be as a landing ground for a manned earth satellite. If this is the case and the project is successful, it will make them very nearly world powerful. A nasty possibility.

'On the other hand, it may be something quite different, we

11

don't know. We haven't enough evidence at the moment one way or the other.

'What we'd better do at the moment is this: I want you, Igor, to go through your files of the last six months and pick out anything that seems to be remotely connected either with the Arctic or with Ittursk. Get hold of all recently arrived émigrés and see if any of them know anything at all about the area. I want to know everything about it, however trivial it seems, from the wind currents to the population of the smallest village.

'When you've done that we'll have a further talk. In the meantime I think we had better have a few more people in on it. I'll call a meeting the day after tomorrow and we'll get all the experts we can. Green from the American Embassy and a few boffins from the research establishments. They might help.

'Till tomorrow then, my dear chap!'

*

When the Russian had left him he sat silently at the table staring at the picture of the dead agent. He did not even look up as his secretary came into the room.

'Excuse me, General,' he said, 'but this was just sent over from the Board of Trade, they thought it might interest us.'

It was a copy of a brief official notice received from the Russian Admiralty. It stated that the White Sea was forthwith closed to all foreign shipping.

'Yes,' said Kirk, half to himself and half to the face in the photograph, 'yes, as you told us, the area is said to be expanding.'

The sun beat on the closed windows and the fire glowed in the grate. His two fingers drummed softly on the table.

'Expanding,' he said again—

*

That night they destroyed the village of Bacharitza.

They destroyed it utterly from the meanest wooden hut to the new concrete loading ramps. They destroyed the houses and the streets and the church and the government offices. They razed it to the ground so that nothing was left of it.

The Commandant stood on a little hillock overlooking the plain and his face was grey with fatigue.

Below and to the left of him were the trucks groaning southward with their pitiful load of refugees. Before him stood the village, and behind was the roar of the oncoming planes.

He turned and looked at them, and they were tight red wedges against the setting sun. His eyes were very proud as he watched them, for they were his planes, the planes that the people had built.

They came over in three unhurried waves and they blasted the village. He was sad too as he watched them, for it was in a sense his village as well. A village of the people.

The dust clouds had died down and the last fire was a small flickering glow in the darkness when he turned and walked away to his waiting car. There was a fear in his eyes which had nothing to do with his military duties.

CHAPTER TWO

WITH a sigh of relief, for she hated housework, Marcia put the last dried cup on the shelf, and went back into the sitting room, lighting a cigarette and looking out of the sunlit window at the towering cathedral.

Durford had never been a great university but it was eminently respectable.

Third in age to Oxford and Cambridge, it had started as a small settlement attached to the cathedral. With the industrial revolution, the town had grown and with it the University. The first small college, begrudgingly founded for technology, had spread to a mass of bright red buildings, of every style of architectural perversity, and far outshadowing the original centre.

Unlike most provincial universities, however, Durford still had a centre. A square of mellow Jacobean houses huddled beneath the gigantic loom of the cathedral and surrounding a grassed quad.

It was across this quad that Marcia was looking. She had only been in Durford three months and this part of it still seemed unbelievably beautiful. On the grass before her, large, self-important cats paced on errands of magnitude, while high up, almost specks in the evening sky, rooks wheeled and soared round the fantastic towers of the cathedral. From the room above came the rattle of a typewriter as her husband Tony Heath, Fellow in biology, finished his notes for tomorrow's lectures.

13

She was very happy. And yet, as she smoked and listened and stared at the towers and the cats and the mellow houses, she felt vaguely uneasy.

How long would Tony stand it! He had seemed settled and contented enough at first, but at their tea party today she had sensed his restlessness growing.

He had done well, making polite conversation to the dowdy, elderly women and listening to the hundred times told anecdotes of the men, but she had felt his irritation.

Although he never admitted it, she was sure he considered this post at Durford a mere backwater, and she supposed he was right. Yet she shuddered as she remembered the last two years.

The frenzy of excitement when he had been offered the post of chief assistant at Farhill, and the frenzy of work that had followed.

How she had loathed those two years. The dates that were always broken, the holidays that were postponed, the nights alone in their big bed. And at the ring of the telephone, always the same message at the end of the line.

'Look, my sweet, I'm terribly sorry about this evening, but something has just cropped up and Hearn and I think we ought to get on with it. No, don't bother to leave anything on the table, we'll have sandwiches sent up here. Right oh, darling, you go to bed and I'll be back as soon as we're through. Good-night, darling.'

But they were never through. It would sometimes be days before she saw him, and each time he would seem more haggard, more strung up, and a little older than his thirty-two years.

This easy post at Durford had seemed a haven to her. They had a house. Tony's work was light and he was mostly at home. Above all they were free from the constant demands of Hearn, the Farhill director.

Yet in a way it was wrong. Tony's work here was almost purely routine. The most brilliant mind that the research station had ever had was relegated to a mere teaching post.

The cathedral suddenly seemed cheap and sham in the evening sky, like a stage set. Below it lay the grim slums of the town and the murky dock area. Behind them were the forgotten, distressed mining villages and beyond the Pennines.

This square with its green lawns, its canons' houses, and its air of fading academic gentility was strangely false and divorced from anything that was real.

She considered the party and her guests. The Dean and the Bursar with their high-pitched, twittering laughter and nervous, crushed wives. Willis and Routledge, the history dons, red faced and hearty, and Roberts, her husband's immediate superior. Poor Roberts ; except for a short wartime break, thirty years at Durford, grey and haggard and followed everywhere by his cretinous daughter.

She thought ahead ; another ten years and she saw herself still keeping the odd tea party. Her hair a little grey perhaps, her body a little thicker, laughing over the cups at the same jokes to the same faces, and out of the corner of her eye, watching Tony slowly conforming to the Durford pattern.

With a click of annoyance she banished these thoughts from her mind and turned from the window ; thus missing the sight of the pennon-bearing Daimler which was slowly entering the square.

At the peal of the bell, she went to the door wondering which of her guests had left gloves or stick behind. As she walked through the little hall, she had a slight feeling of uneasiness. It was nothing. Just a vague, distant, very far off feeling that something was wrong. It was so slight that it didn't trouble her for a second. It was only a fleeting glimpse and she paid no attention to it. But all the same it might have been a premonition of the thing that was coming.

*

The man on the step was six foot one and he looked squat. He had a dark suit and a dark tie with a nice gold pin in it. He held his dark hat in his hand and his leather gloves made his hands look enormous. His face was hearty and red and his eyes twinkled. He might have been a high class bookmaker. But he was no bookmaker, he was Dr. Walter Hearn.

'My dear Mrs. Heath.' The voice was rich and fruity and the hand that held hers was very firm.

'My dear Mrs. Heath, how nice to see you again, how very nice. I'm most terribly sorry to call on you like this without letting you know first, but I'm sure you'll understand.'

'Of course Doctor Hearn, I'm sure Tony'll be delighted to see you. Do come in.'

She led him through into the sitting-room and he made it look tiny. He placed his dark hat on the table and looked around him. He looked at her, and the room and the view through the window and beamed at everything.

'But, my dear, this is charming, quite charming.' His circling arm seemed to take in all there was. The room, the square, the cathedral, all of Durford life.

'And you and Tony, my dear, how are you both? I don't

15

suppose they work him as hard here as I did.' He smiled for a moment, and then was suddenly serious.

'It's about work I want to see him really. No, my dear, don't worry. I'm not going to ask him to come back to Farhill, however much I would like to. I know what a hard time you both had and I'm sure things are much better for you here. No, it's nothing like that. It's just, how shall I put it, just a slight favour I want him to do for me. It won't take long, only a day, I promise you.'

'But of course, Doctor, I'm sure he'll help if he can. I'll go and tell him you're here.' Her voice was full of relief for she was sure that if he had asked Tony to go back to Farhill he would have accepted.

She turned and ran up the stairs to fetch her husband.

Left alone in the little room, Hearn fingered his immaculate tie and ran his hand softly over his crisp grey hair. He stroked the gilt bindings in the bookcase and beamed at everything. Yet for all his pomposity, his urbanity, his beaming manner, his eyes were very shrewd.

He turned to the door as hurried footsteps came down the stairs and held out his hand to his former colleague.

'Hearn, by all that's wonderful ; how are you? Marcia told me we had a visitor, but I never thought it would be you, this is delightful. Come over here and sit down, and I'll get you a drink.'

Although much shorter than the director, Tony's slim build made their height seem equal. He was an untidy young man, more through impatience than inclination, and his face seemed to be perpetually working with new ideas. He was obviously delighted to see Hearn. As she came into the room behind him Marcia noted the excitement in his face, as he went to the sideboard.

He handed round the sherry and then looked at Hearn. 'Well, old man, what is it? Not a social call, all the way from London, surely.'

'No, Tony, sorry, but much as I would have liked it, not a social call.' The big man leaned forward in his chair and his voice was rich and beautifully modulated.

'The fact is I'm in a jam. Nothing much, but it could be embarrassing. Young Clift, who took your place. A brilliant boy in his way, quite brilliant, he's going to be all right, but at the moment he's just a little lacking in experience.' He put the glass to his lips and sipped the sherry before continuing.

'Well, to put it briefly I had a phone call from Kirk this morning. You may have heard of General Kirk, my dear,' he said to Marcia. 'A very important man ; I can't afford to

16

offend him. It seems he is calling a conference tomorrow. He gave no details but it is to be absolutely top level. All the other departments are to be brought in as well as ours and it's all very hush hush. Well that's put me in a spot. I've got Hughes away on holiday; can't get him back on time and Kirk said he wanted somebody absolutely conversant with the latest advances in germ warfare, and especially Russian advances. Well, Tony, I think that means you.'

'So, Kirk suddenly calls a conference at a moment's notice, does he?' said Tony slowly. 'How very interesting; it's so unlike him. I wonder why.

'You know, my dear chap, I'd love to help you, but I don't think I can. I mean after all, I've been away from the place for over two months, I'll be hopelessly out of touch with the situation.'

'Yes, I realize that, that's why I wondered.' He looked appealingly at Marcia. 'I wondered if you could come up with me tonight, and we could go through the new stuff together. There's not a lot and I could put you in the picture, so you'd be quite up to it in the morning.'

'Don't worry, Doctor, he'll go.' Marcia stood up and crossed to her husband, putting her hand on his shoulder. 'He'll go if he has to crawl there on his knees. I know him. Now don't argue, darling. I don't mind a little fling now and again; though I think I might leave you if you went back to work for him permanently.'

Tony lifted her hand and kissed the palm.

'Thank you, sweet, but it's not only that. You see, Hearn, these people here have been pretty decent to me and I don't honestly think I can let them down. I've got two lectures tomorrow and I can't just walk out the day before. No, sorry, but I think it'll have to be Clift after all.'

'But surely, surely there is somebody who can take your place. After all, Kirk is important. Can't these wretched students find someone else to lecture to them?'

'Of course they can, Tony,' Marcia broke in. 'Roberts will do it, he'll be delighted to, he more or less implied that if ever you felt you had too much to do he would help. After all, as you told me, it's just routine stuff. I'm sure he'll do it if I ask him.'

She paused and took up a small blue note-book from the desk. 'His address is in here, that poor idiot daughter of his made me take it down this afternoon. It's somewhere near the docks; funny place for a professor to live, but that's his business. I'll get your things together.' She turned and went out of the room.

17

'What a wife!' said Hearn, 'what a wife! Well, my boy, there's no excuse for you now and don't worry, I'll see you're back tomorrow. Got the address?'

'Yes, number five Sunderland Street; as she says, a funny area. Right you are, old man, I'll come with you. We'll drop Marcia by the bridge, it's near there. I'll just go up and give her a hand with my things.'

*

The big, smooth car purred soundlessly down the steep streets and halted at the end of the bridge. Marcia got out and kissed Tony.

'Good luck, darling. Get this fellow Kirk sorted out and don't overdo it. But remember I want you back tomorrow. All right, off you go.'

She watched the car cross the bridge and disappear among the grey streets beyond it and then turned back and began to walk towards Sunderland Street.

In a way she was happy, for although Tony had gone, this trip would give him a chance to let off steam and she hoped he might be more settled when he returned.

But as she walked along the road towards Sunderland Street, she began to feel terribly alone, as she looked around her.

Durford is a city of contrasts.

High up on the top of the hill rest the cathedral and the centre of the University, secure and comfortable, the heirs of the Middle Ages and culture.

A little below are the modern colleges and the shopping centre, mainly Victorian, but since the bombing bearing a pattern of white concrete.

Below them all is the old town.

There is nothing ancient or historical about Durford Old Town. Once perhaps a legion might have encamped by the fords and once a Saxon village had stood on the bank of the river, but the present old town is purely nineteenth century.

It is an area of steep narrow streets and tall narrow houses, straggling up from the docks and the dank river as if reaching for light on the more favoured slopes of the hill.

Dark houses, soot-blackened from the railways and the ships and mines. Identical houses in identical streets that each bear the name of a town and the marks of decay and neglect and despair. Identical except for one or two of them which stand back from the others; a little larger, a little more pretentious, a little more decorative. Houses of forgotten merchants and manufacturers who liked to live near their work, but whose sons had moved up into the air and left them as forlorn as the rest of the area.

'Why!' thought Marcia as she moved through the blackened streets, 'why should a man like Roberts, a senior professor of the University, live in a place like this?'

Beside her a tram lurched and thundered northward up the hill and in the distance a ship's siren howled, immensely sad in the fading daylight.

There were nasty stories about the place. A year ago women had been known to disappear here. Some of them had come to light weeks later, fish and fly torn in the stagnant river. Others had just vanished. There had been no arrest or suspects.

There were chalk drawings on the walls on both sides. One of them so horrible, and yet so sad in its implied deformity that she hurried on shuddering.

Ragged children shook their heads as she asked them the way and then pointed shyly forwards.

At last she came to it. A soot-covered sign, Sunderland Street, and number five tall and gaunt in front of her.

Because of its size and air of long lost prosperity, the house appeared almost more woebegone than its neighbours. It seemed older, too, not old with any pleasant hoariness, but just old. Old with the terrible age of neglect.

It stood back a little way from the road, behind iron railings and an overgrown ruin of a garden. The stucco work was cracked and mouldering and the paint on the brown door was peeling.

She lifted the heavy, old-fashioned lever on the wall, and far away in the back of the house a bell jangled.

For a long time she waited on the step and no one came.

Men in cloth caps, tugging greyhounds, grinned as they passed her, and at the end of the street a motor-cycle started explosively. Again she tugged at the bell pull, and at last, very far away in the distance, a door banged and a board creaked and slow, hesitant steps began to come towards her.

There was a sound of a bolt being withdrawn and the rattle of a chain as the door partly opened, but only partly.

From the gloom inside, Marcia saw two frightened eyes looking at her behind spectacles, and a very frightened voice spoke to her.

'Please go away,' said the voice, 'please go away, I'm very sorry, but I can't let you in. I'm not allowed to let anybody in and Daddy's working, he can't see anyone.'

'It's all right, Miss Roberts, it's only me, Mrs. Heath. You

19

remember me, don't you, you came to our party today. Don't be frightened, I just want to speak to your father for a moment.'

'Oh, Mrs. Heath ; yes, how silly of me, I remember the party. We had cream cakes, didn't we, and you live in the quad. I wish we lived in the quad, I hate it here. The children shout at me when I go out alone and there are rats in the house. I hate rats ; once one jumped at me. I wish we had a cat. I love cats, but Daddy doesn't like them. I wish I could let you in, Mrs. Heath, I like you, but Daddy says I mustn't let anyone in unless he says so and mustn't disturb him in the evenings. Once I let some boys and they—'

Rather horribly the voice broke off into a giggle.

'Miss Roberts, Mary isn't it?' For one unhappy term, Marcia had taught in a board school and she tried to bring back the old, accustomed firmness.

'Mary, there is nothing at all for you to worry about, but I must see your father for a moment. Please let me in, or tell him I'm here.'

There was a pause and then she heard the chain being withdrawn, the door opened and she stepped into the hall.

The house was a brown house. Everything about it was brown from the dull brown paint on the woodwork to the brown wallpaper hung with faded brown lithographs. From every side of her, lovers in sepia took their last ride together and girls in crinolines played with pugs. Even the dress of the trembling creature before her was a dull lustreless brown.

Marcia looked at her and she was sad as she looked. Sad for the slight body with one arm shorter than the other. Sad for the frightened eyes behind the glasses and the trembling slack lips. Sad above all for the shining auburn hair that shone beautiful in the gloom like a mockery over the white expressionless flesh of her face.

'Thank you, Mary,' she said, 'that's much better, now run and tell your father I've come to see him for a minute.'

Above her head a door slammed and there was a sound of steps on the landing.

'What is it, Mary, who have you got there?' The figure of the Professor stood at the top of the stairs peering short-sightedly down at them. 'How many times must I tell you not to open the door to anyone? Oh, it's you, Mrs. Heath, I'm so sorry but I didn't recognize you. I'm afraid my eyes are not at all what they should be.'

He hurried down the stairs, his slippers flapping loosely on the treads. 'I'm afraid I must have frightened you shouting like that, but since those poor women disappeared we have

20

to be so careful round here. Terrible business, really terrible.'
He held out his hand to her and then motioned her across the
hall. 'But what am I thinking of. Come through into the
drawing-room, my dear. This way.

'Mary, run and bring a glass of sherry for our guest.'

The drawing-room had once been very feminine, but that
was long ago. The patterned wallpaper and the decorative
furniture covers were dull and faded. The china stood in
cupboards, dirty and uncared for. The very chair she sat in
was grey with dust.

'I must ask you to excuse this room, Mrs. Heath, we hardly
ever seem to use it now.' The eyes were tired and sad behind
the glasses.

'When my wife was alive now, we used to have such a lot of
visitors. Ah! here you are, Mary. A glass of sherry, my dear.'

He poured her a glass of dark sickly liquid and then leaned
back opposite her.

'Now, what can I do for you?'

Very briefly Marcia explained the situation and watched
his eyes light up with curiosity.

'I see, but how very interesting. Of course I knew all about
your husband's last post before he came to Durford. But this
is most exciting. No details of course, and you couldn't tell me
anything if there were. But it must have been something most
important for the director himself to come down all the way
from London, and at such short notice. I do wonder what it
can be.

'One feels so out of touch with things here. It really is
refreshing to have a man like your husband with us, my dear.
But don't you worry, I'll look after the honours course, and
the first year will just have to look after itself. They won't
mind.' He chuckled dryly and raised his glass to his lips. 'Well,
my dear, here's success to your husband's venture, whatever it
may be.'

Marcia forced herself to drink the thick over-sweet sherry
and thanked him for his help. For a little while she chatted
and then rose to leave.

In the hall she paused and turned to him, struck by something she had noticed when she first came in. Although the
house was full of dirt and damp and neglect, there was all over
it a sweet almost overpowering odour blotting out all the
smells of rot and dust.

'Professor Roberts,' she said, 'what is it, this scent, it's so
pleasant?'

'Ah, I can see you're not a Catholic, my dear. It's incense
of course. I'm afraid I'm not a very good churchman, but it

gives me a little comfort, you know. Since these terrible murders I've felt that it is almost as if a curse hangs over this neighbourhood. Sometimes I long to move from here but somehow my wife's memory always keeps me. Besides, I'm an old dog now. Too old to start again somewhere else.'

He opened the door and then looked seriously at her. 'Mrs. Heath,' he said, and his words were very solemn. 'Mrs. Heath, please don't think I'm impertinent, but I like you, and I would, if I might, give you a little advice. Don't stay long at Durford ; whatever you think now it's not good for you or your husband. Leave soon, before you both become as stale as I am. It's no good for you.'

He turned on his heels and almost slammed the door in her face.

She turned slowly from the doorway and walked down the overgrown path, surprised and shocked at his words. As she reached the gate she looked back and could see him standing watching her from the window, the slim figure of Mary at his side.

Although it was the height of summer and still hot, clouds were high over the town and it was getting dark.

She walked home briskly, breathing in the evening air and feeling refreshed after the musty old house.

She passed small pubs and lighted shops piled high with grey mounds of tripe. She walked under looming warehouses with the dark shapes of ships behind them. Then up the hill to the traffic and the neon signs and the branches of the London stores, and as she walked she thought of the Daimler purring south under the soft Lincolnshire sky with Tony and Hearn.

In the square the cathedral no longer seemed beautiful but brooded over the town of contrasts, as shapeless as one of its own gargoyles. Below the neat square stood the tall house she had just visited, and the pubs and the tripe shops and the despair of the forgotten, unused drawing-room.

She drew her jacket closer round her and almost ran across the grass to her front door.

For a few minutes she tried to settle down in a chair and read, but it was no good. The sense of loneliness was too strong and she was also immensely curious.

Why should Hearn suddenly call for Tony like this? What did this General want that was so important, that a permanent official could not deal with? Why did they need the services of a research biologist? Why should Roberts warn her against Durford?

She got up and went into the kitchen for a cup of tea.

As she came back into the room the cathedral clock was

beginning to strike. Cup in hand she switched on the radio for the news summary.

With the last stroke of the clock, beautifully clear and modulated, the well-bred voice filled the room.

'In the House of Lords today, the Archbishops have spoken on the abolition of the Death Penalty.

'The M.C.C. beat the West African touring eleven by an innings and thirty-two runs. Yeates took eight wickets for sixty-five runs.

'Moscow Radio announces the temporary closure of its White Sea ports to foreign shipping.'

She turned off the radio and once more tried to interest herself in the novel.

CHAPTER THREE

THE White Sea may sometimes be white; it is usually green. That night it was grey.

The hot air from the sun-parched land-mass had met the cold Arctic currents and a thick fog hung over the water.

Through the fog came the British steamer *Gadshill*.

The lookout stood on the forecastle head and he was almost blind in the fog. At his side he could just make out the dark bulk of the donkey engine and that was all. Below him came the soughing of the water round her bows, and behind the dull beat of the engines, running at half speed. Every sixty seconds the siren roared horribly, and during the intervals the air was alive with small noises as the old ship creaked and groaned in the swell.

For the *Gadshill* was very old. The fog hid her scars and peeling paint and stove pipe funnel, and the old men who manned her.

Everything about her was old from her rusty, pitted plates to her superannuated officers. She had been torn and twisted in two wars and battered by a thousand storms. She had rotted and mouldered in tropical rivers and above all the long, useless years of the depression had eaten into her soul. Even the rats who swarmed in her leaking holds seemed aged and dispirited.

Now she was going home. After she had unloaded this cargo of timber she would move down river to the breakers, and that would be the end of her. Her steel would go into other ships. Her officers would be pensioned off and she would be forgotten. It was odd that at this moment she was about to make history.

On her bridge, slight, whiskered, and cantankerous stomped her master, Capt. Adolphus Miles Clarke, O.B.E.

'Bluddy 'ell,' he muttered, partly to himself and partly to the shadowy figure of the mate beside him.

'Well, this is a bluddy fine start to our last voyage, Mister. First the bluddy Russians order us out of Archangel three days before schedule ; only two-thirds of our cargo on board and no bluddy rhyme or reason given for it either. What the company'll say about it I don't know. And now this bluddy fog.'

He flapped his arms against his steaming oilskin and thought of the events of the day.

It had started at seven o'clock when he had received an urgent summons from the second officer. He had come grumbling on deck from his snug cabin and received his first surprise. The huge wooden dock, usually teeming with workers, was bare and deserted, save for the sentry solemnly pacing beside the ship.

At first Clarke had not been concerned. It appeared that the night shift had left at six, half an hour earlier than usual, and no relief had arrived.

He had not worried much about it. Dockers were the same idle, troublesome lot the world over and these were Bolshevik dockers. They'd be back soon, he thought, this was just a delay. Probably a deliberate effort to cause inconvenience to himself and cut down the rightful profits of Messrs. Tupper and Jacobsen, the *Gadshill*'s owners.

At ten o'clock his complacency had been rudely shattered.

A large Russian Packard blazoned with flags and emblems had rolled majestically along the dock and halted at the gangway. From it had stepped the superintendent, whom he knew, and a tall officer wearing a deceptively quiet uniform.

He had taken them down to his cabin and offered whisky, as he did to any foreigner bearing a vestige of authority, and in five minutes the situation was clear to him.

By three o'clock that afternoon the *Gadshill* was to leave Archangel. Major Malendof, for that was the tall officer's name, was very polite about it. He expressed his own great personal regret at this order, but Capt. Clarke would realize that he was merely a servant of his government. The fact was that Archangel had become part of a restricted area, and it was his responsibility to see that all foreign shipping left it by the time specified.

Capt. Clarke raged and stormed. He pointed out the dire

consequences that his expulsion would incur. He threatened to appeal to his owners, the British government, the United Nations if necessary. But it was to no avail. Malendof was adamant.

He saw how very inconvenient it was for them to leave at such short notice. He realized the losses which would be incurred by Messrs. Tupper and Jacobsen if the ship sailed without her full cargo, but doubtless the government, noted for its generosity, would pay full compensation. In any case his orders were clear. From three o'clock the area was closed to all foreign vessels. He could give no reasons for this ; as he had said, he was merely a subordinate. Tugs would be put at their disposal at two to assist them down the river and he was sure Capt. Clarke would co-operate with him. In the case of non-compliance, he was sorry but he had to inform him that the ship would be taken over by the military and the crew sent home by air. He was certain that the owners would not welcome this alternative.

Now he had to go. Although the *Gadshill* was the only foreign vessel in the port he had a great many other duties to attend to. As he had said, he was personally very sorry and would like to wish them a very good voyage home. The tugs would be alongside in good time and he knew Capt. Clarke's better judgement would prevail. The weather was reported to be calm for the area. He bowed stiffly and walked out to his waiting car.

They left. There was nothing else they could do. Punctual to the minute the tugs snorted alongside and a lorry-load of soldiers drew up before the gangway. At two fifteen Clarke's hand reached for the telegraph.

So they went to sea. A tug fore and aft and curses and sweat from the engine-room staff took them down the river, and an hour later they met the first oily swells of the Gulf of Archangel.

*

The evening watches were just changing when they reached the fog. At first it was a slight mist which did not trouble them and with steam up the old ship rolled proudly on at her full nine knots. Gradually it thickened and closed round them, shortening visibility to a few yards, and at last fell like a curtain on all sides.

Clarke crossed to the wheel-house and peered over the lighted compass, then he walked back to the mate.

'Well, Mister, you'll be all right now, I think. It'll be as thick as hell for hours but there's no traffic about worth mentioning, and we're well off the land. I'm going below for a bit. I've got my log to finish and I want to write a report for Sparks to send to the Company. What the directors'll say about this'll be nobody's business. Ruddy international incident I shouldn't wonder. International incident.' He savoured the words with pleasure and then turned and went below to his cabin.

It was snug below. He kept the door tightly closed and the air was free from fog. He looked with satisfaction around the dingy box that had been his home for twenty years, and then sat down at the stained battered desk to begin the agreeable task of putting his complaints on paper.

Outside the fog held the steamer like dark grey cloth. The mate peered in front of him and his reddened eyes saw nothing. The water lapped slowly along the battered sides and the steam roared through the siren, as at half revolutions the engines shuddered on through the darkness.

Not for long was Clarke allowed his report. A little before seven bells he knew that something was wrong. It was nothing definite at first. Just a vague feeling that kept creeping through the back of his head as he bent over the paper. All around him were the familiar shipboard noises and, above, the muffled howl of the siren.

He put down his pen and listened and then suddenly was on his feet, drawing his oilskins around him.

As he opened the door, the speaking tube sounded by his bunk, but he didn't stop to answer it, moving out of his cabin and along the companionway as fast as his years permitted.

The mate was in the wheel-house in earnest conversation with the quartermaster. He straightened as Clarke came towards him.

'Glad you've come, sir, did you hear 'em?'

'Them! I heard a ship, Mister Grove, a big 'un, by the sound of 'er, and going fast. Any idea what she was?'

'There was more than one, sir, three at least. Warships by the sound of 'em and going like 'ell; the murderous bastards. Right on the port quarter. Not a dozen ruddy fathoms in it.'

'Umph! I see. Well, we seem to be through 'em, but just in case.' He picked up the bridge telephone and bawled at the lookouts. 'You men, Smith and Daniels; as you know, there are ships about. I want you to get your flares going till we're sure we're through 'em.'

He dropped the instrument back on to its hook and listened. The *Gadshill*'s siren tore again through the fog, and as it stopped the two men on the bridge stiffened.

26

There was another sound in the air now. Very faint and far away in the distance something was coming towards them. They could hear a movement of broken water that was not their own, and a deep slow drone that could only be the drone of a turbine. It was coming fast. At every second the slapping water was closer and the hum louder.

The two old men stood close together on the swaying bridge, their hands almost touching as they leaned forward on the rail, desperately trying to discover the course of the oncoming vessel, and each of them dreaded a death he could not see.

And then suddenly they saw it. The fog lifted for a fraction of a second and she was there. A bow like a cliff was up on the swell to starboard with white water in front of it, as it pointed towards them. With a cry that was drowned by an enormous siren that was not the *Gadshill's*, Clarke hurled himself at the wheel. His fingers clawed madly at the spokes. Every ounce of strength in his old body went on to that spinning wheel. He felt her answer to it, answer and swing wildly to port, felt that he had succeeded and then knew that it was too late.

The collision itself was almost gentle. Just a quick tearing sound and a slight tremor and then the newcomer was gone, and they were alone. The old ship seemed to sway softly, almost normally, in the passing wash as if uninjured, and then she began to die.

There was a crash of breaking, tortured metal as the bulkheads collapsed. The roar of escaping steam and above all a rush of water. For a moment all was pandemonium. Men who a few seconds past had been sleeping came rushing on deck, screaming and cursing, blinded by fog and steam. From the engine-room, nobody came.

After a time some semblance of order was obtained. The electrical apparatus still worked and, with orders from the loudspeakers, the crew got to their boat stations and the officers gathered in the chart room.

Clarke straightened himself from the table and turned to his Chief Engineer.

'Well, Mr. McAdam, how long have we got?'

The Chief was as indifferent as if he was considering some minor fault in his precious engines. He put a blackened pipe to his lips, fumbled in his pyjama pocket for matches, and slowly lit it before replying.

'Weel, Captain Clarke, ah hev noo wish to commit meself, but it's me considered opinion that she'll go doon in fifteen minits at the verra outside. It's only the timber that is keeping her afloat at all; with any ither cargo she would have sunk by now. The engine-room is flooded as is number three hold. As soon as the water rises far enough to bairst the after bulkhead she'll go.'

'Thank you, Chief. Well, gentlemen, I am abandoning ship in five minutes. There appears to be a fishing village to the south-south-east of us. We'll head for it. The boats will try to keep together and will burn flares. The murderous devils may be looking for us, though I doubt it.

'Sparks, send out your SOS again and give details of the collision. Then get to your boat. All right, you can all go to your stations now. I'll join you in five minutes.'

For the last time he looked at the chart-room where he had held sway for twenty years. He ran his hand over the sextant in its gleaming brass case, and looked at the chronometer on the table.

So this was the parting of the ways. He felt no sorrow, though he would have liked to take her home. Still, this was, in a sense, a better end than the Jarrow hammers.

There was only one thing more for him to do. He walked down to his room and very carefully packed into his water-proof case the unfinished log, and a framed photograph of a plain woman leaning beside a terrace wall. He spared not a glance for his cabin, his furniture or anything that was left, but walked out, very stiffly, very firmly, very much the master of a ship, to the waiting boats.

So the *Gadshill* sank. There was no other way to describe it, she just sank.

No band played 'Nearer, my God, to thee' from her rusty deck. No soldiers stood stiffly to attention. No ray of sunlight lit up the name on her stern. She just sank and only the floating dead in the engine-room saw her go.

From the boats they saw nothing. All that told them of her end was a sudden heaving of the water around them and deep splashes, as timber shot to the surface and fell again. All they knew was that they were alone.

For half an hour they managed to keep together, and then swell and fog separated them and they worked on by their own navigation. In the leading boat with Clarke, the wireless operator struggled with his transmitter and received no reply. The oars rose and fell over the water and the prow bobbed on through the blanket of fog, as they rowed to the shore.

There was nothing horrible in their situation. They knew that land was not far off, but what would they find when they reached it? They were rowing towards a forbidden territory from which they had just been expelled. They thought there was a village in front of them, but if they were wrong they

28

would be cut off from life by miles of barren tundra marsh. If they did find the village, what would their reception be?

But they rowed on. There was nothing else they could do. For hour after hour they rowed and still the fog showed no sign of lifting. It was all round them like walls and even the falling oar blades were invisible. Their lungs seemed filled with cotton wool and their eyes streamed and ached, as they rowed to the coast. The coast of the restricted area.

*

About daybreak they reached it. There was no sign of day. The fog was as thick as ever, if slightly more white than grey. At first they smelt the seaweed and the salt odour of the land. Then from time to time came the sound of lapping water. And at last the boat lifted with the swell, and slid heavily on to mud.

For a moment no one spoke, and then Clarke moved from the tiller and went to the centre of the boat.

'Well, Sparks, any luck with that thing yet?'

The wireless operator shook his head. 'No luck at all, sir. I can hear one or two Russian stations very faint, but nothing concerning us. I don't think there's anybody near enough for me to reach with this contraption; it's only got a fifty mile radius, you know.'

'I see, well all the same, go on trying as long as your battery lasts. Now, lads,' he turned to the rest of the crew. 'We're going to sit here for a while till this fog lifts. It's bound to do so in time, and we're quite comfortable here. If we start blundering off into that marsh, God knows what will happen to us. We've got food and drink, and most of us have had some slight experience of sitting in lifeboats, so let's stay put for a bit. All right, steward, you can break out some more brandy.'

So they sat and waited for the fog to lift, but it showed no sign of lifting. At the end of three hours Clarke looked at his watch and knew that he had to make a move.

He had two wounded men in the boat and their groans were getting fainter. He hated the idea of leaving the boat, of walking off through the fog to the hidden coast, but it had to be done.

He heaved himself to his feet.

'Well, I think it's time some of us went for a little walk now,' he said slowly. 'If the village is over there, we'll try and get some help. If not, there'll be no harm done. This is the idea. I want two men to come with me. We'll tie ourselves together so there'll be no fear of getting separated. While we're gone I want you, French, to get up in the bows and keep working that hand siren. I want it turned three times every thirty

29

seconds. Got that, three times, every thirty seconds. We'll keep going as long as we can hear the siren easily, and then if there is no village we'll be able to get back to the boat. All right, then, who's coming with me? Very well, I'll take you, Knight, and you, Jackson. You'll be in command here, Mr. McAdam, while we're gone. Now pass me some line out of the locker, and we'll get going.'

With difficulty the three men waded to the shore. The going was slow and wearisome. The mud was soft and undulating, and gave no grip to their boots. Sometimes it sank with them and they struggled up to the waist in water, jerked and hampered by the line. Every thirty seconds the horn spoke to them like a voice of comfort in the fog.

Suddenly they were there. The ground shelved slightly, became harder. The water dropped and they were walking on firm, dry tundra. They paused and looked around them, seeing nothing except their own faces as pale as tallow.

'Well, we'll try to the right first,' said Clarke, 'there's no point in going inland. If there is a village it's bound to be near the water. We'll go as far to the right as we can, and then try the other way. Let's go.'

For hours they seemed to walk. The ground was hard and brittle and rang like iron beneath their feet. Apart from the thin covering of moss there seemed to be no vegetation. It was a dead, lifeless land which might have been covered by fog for ever. They walked slowly, moving their feet with care, holding their hands before their faces and straining against the line that held them together. Each one of them listened to the sound of the boat's siren, and thought longingly of the companionship of their fellows, huddled on the benches. They must have been walking round some bay or estuary, for as they walked the horn seemed to get no fainter. On and on they went, step after weary step, hands groping before them; only the tug of the rope and the ring of their feet told them they were not alone.

Suddenly the rope jerked sharply. Clarke and Knight were almost pulled to the ground as Jackson stopped.

'Arf a minute, sir; sorry to stop dead like that, but listen.' They listened. They listened to their own breathing, to the water lapping on the shore, to the wail of the river, but that was all.

'It seems to have stopped now, sir, but I could 'ave sworn there was something when we was coming along just now. Like something being dragged behind us, sir. Quite close it sounded, sir.'

'Well, there's nothing now, man, anyway. You've been

letting your mind play tricks with you,' said Clarke. 'Come on let's get on.'

'No, beg pardon, sir, but I think there is something!' It was Knight who spoke this time. 'It seems to be thinning a bit over here. There's something over to me right. Yes, I can see it, sir. Just there.'

Very cautiously they approached the dark shape before them, and slowly it began to take form. With a cry of triumph Knight tugged madly on the rope and dragged them towards it.

'We've made it, sir, your navigation was orl right, sir, we'll be fixed up now, sir. Here, you inside,' he shouted, 'friends, tovarish, help, open up!' His gnarled fist beat on the door of the rickety wooden hut that loomed gaunt and forbidding before them. There was obviously no one there. After a time they gave up shouting and tried the handle. The door opened easily and they went inside.

In the hut the air was clearer and they could see. They looked round the interior and stared in amazement. For it was a shambles.

'Well,' said Clarke softly, 'whoever lived here certainly left in a hurry.' He felt fear coming gently towards him as he spoke.

The ruin of the hut was extraordinary. Every piece of rough furniture was in disorder. A table lay on its side, half covered by a piece of torn blanket. A chest stood in the corner and its drawers lay on the floor beside it, spilling worthless possessions on the ground. Everywhere there was broken glass and china, and above all there was something they remembered. An atmosphere, a feeling, an odour. Something familiar and yet indefinable.

'Cor, sir,' muttered Jackson, 'something must have put the wind up the blighters to make 'em leave like this.'

Clarke nodded and examined the room. He poked through the littered drawers and cupboards, trying to find something that would give him an inkling of what had happened. But there was no clue, and fear was very close to him now.

After a time he led them out of the hut and they went on. For a few yards more they groped through the fog and soon he knew that his navigation was right. They were in a village. They counted ten huts. They examined ten huts, and every hut was exactly the same. The same broken crockery and littered possessions, the same overturned furniture. The marks of flight.

After they had inspected the last hut they turned and walked back to the boat. They didn't speak or discuss their departure. Clarke gave no orders. They merely turned like one man on the rope and walked away; for each one of them knew that there was now only one thing in the whole universe that was important to him. To get away from that deserted, ransacked village.

They walked slowly back to the boat and fear was with them at each step. Whatever had made the Russians leave like that had been something sudden. There was no sign of system. No planned evacuation, but a sudden mad rush. A hurried grabbing of possessions, a rummaging among drawers, a pulling over of furniture, and flight. 'What is the thing that is bad enough to make people behave like that?' said Fear, through the fog.

What? As he groped forward Clarke kept thinking, what? What could make ten families suddenly desert their homes at a moment's notice? If the authorities had wanted to evacuate the area they would have done it systematically. This had been blind panic. What was the thing that had caused their panic?

He was soon to know. When they were about half way back to the boat, Jackson touched his arm.

'Sir, stop a moment and listen. Behind us, sir. A sort of scraping noise, like I said before, sir.'

Clarke stopped and listened, and this time there was something. It was very faint, scarcely audible, but it was there. A sound of something soft being dragged over the dry marsh.

The three men turned and looked in the direction of the sound, and it was coming nearer. It was soft and faint and far away, but it was coming nearer. Scraping softly over the tundra towards them.

Then it happened. By some trick of air or wind or atmosphere, the fog lifted. It swirled gently upwards in thin wisps, and for a moment they could see.

It was just a glimpse, just a fleeting glance, but it was enough.

They were tough products of the Liverpool docks. They had come through the hardest school in the world, and war and wreck and storm had not touched them. But suddenly they were huddled together like children, crying and whimpering and desperately drawing back as they looked at the thing that the fog had mercifully hidden.

The tide was going out and the boat rocked and groaned as she settled deeper in the mud. Every thirty seconds the horn blared out, but none of the men in the boat thought that there was anybody to hear it.

'Eight ruddy hours,' said the second officer. 'Hell! eight ruddy hours since they left.'

He said Hell, and it meant nothing, he just said it. So they waited in the boat and wound the siren and cursed. They cursed the fog and the cold and the Russian warship and the grinding of the boat's keel in the mud.

The mud across which with every inch of the lowering tide the real Hell was coming towards them.

CHAPTER FOUR

WHEN we are dead, we have no faces. Sometimes we have features that, neat and shaven, stare up from crisp pillows, or leer broken on roads and battlefields. But we have no faces. The dead never have anything that can be called a face.

And Capt. Clarke had not even features. His head lolled on the rough tundra and it was quite smooth. He had no nose, no mouth, no pearls that were his eyes ; he had nothing to distinguish him. But although he was dead, his words were beginning to come true.

'International incident,' he had muttered from the fog-bound deck of the *Gadshill,* and 'International incident' said General Kirk to himself as he came out of the gloomy building that housed his superiors.

Kirk was in a vile temper. He always hated talking to the politicians, and this morning he had been three hours with them.

When he had gone there, he had known how weak his case was, but he had not expected such bland dismissal of the facts he held.

He had been listened to for a few minutes and then had come the lectures. He had been informed on the more promising hopes for peace in the world. The changed attitude of the new Soviet government. The position of Britain as a corner-stone for peace. The need for trust in the present Soviet policy. Cliché had followed cliché, and above all, though they didn't say it, he sensed the real reason for silence ; the forthcoming General Election.

At the end Kirk had reached a compromise. Although it was not enough, he could make them do something. The loss of twenty-five men and a superannuated tramp steamer had given him that chance. They had to act on that. The hurried Russian denial, after the ship's message, had come far too pat for it not to be suspicious. They had to do something.

Tomorrow afternoon, the Foreign Secretary would leave for New York, and take the place of their permanent delegate at the United Nations. He would get up and ask the Russians question after question about the loss of—what was her name —the *Gadshill*.

He wouldn't get any satisfaction, Kirk was sure of that. He could imagine the blank denials, the polite look of disapproval on the bland Muscovite face ; the final lecture on the evils of suspicion and the need for mutual trust. But perhaps as he spoke Yakov might give something away, might make one slight slip which would tell Kirk what was happening on Russia's northern fringe.

Not that he had any real doubt left.

As he waved his waiting car aside and began to walk through the brick forest of Westminster, he was almost sure he knew. His meeting with the experts had convinced him that the satellite was the only possibility.

He thought of the meeting. Six men sitting round a stained table, each with his pad and blotter in front of him.

Six ordinary men, not one of them looked any different from the lunchtime crowds who jostled round him at the moment.

The American, Green, the under secretary, Roach from the Guided missile place, that young chap, Heath, from Farhill, and himself and Trubenoff.

Six men, company directors one could have thought, sitting round the table discussing the firm's assets, and the amount of the new dividend. And so in a sense they were. But if their conclusions were correct there were no assets and no dividend. The assets belonged to the other side. Whoever perfected the satellite would be the undisputed masters of the earth.

Trafalgar Square was sparkling in the bright sunlight, with the plumes of the fountains waving around the pillar of the adulterous admiral, as he watched over the city that had ruined his mistress.

Very faint through the cries of the men selling bird seed and the roar of the traffic, a band was playing in the distance. Kirk looked up through the Admiralty Arch to the green expanse of the Park, alive with flags and flowers, and he thought of another green place, under another sky. It would be a darker more dismal green ; bare of flowers and almost grey in places, where the moss and thin grass was ragged. An empty and desolate place, fringed with trees and grey water. And yet, not quite empty, for something might soon be coming to fill it.

Something out of the sky. Something huge, if Roach the expert had been right. Something that needed three hundred miles to play with. Something that was coming down between Purflu and Karen.

34

He could imagine the thing land. It would be miles out probably, but what did that matter. It had plenty of room. It would lie among broken trees or singed grass and an army of technicians would surround it. They would swarm over it when it was cool and begin to prepare their data on the flight. With that, a few errors could be corrected. The next attempt would be a little more accurate. Still out of course. A hundred miles perhaps, but better.

And so they would carry on. Always improving, always a mile or so nearer the mark, till at last, one fine morning, somebody would be satisfied.

Kirk looked at the milling crowds with distaste and pulled his coat tighter round him. He did not like the city he lived in. He did not like the crowds, the traffic, the noise, or the flickering advertisements. He did not like the giggling girls in jeans who eyed his heavy clothes with amusement. But in his mind he could see this thing coming down over the roofs of the National Gallery and he felt afraid.

They still talked about the Blitz in tubes and buses.

'We had three windows blown out that night,' they said, 'but then London can take it.'

Oh, yes, without a doubt, London could take it. But not this, there was nothing in the world that could take this.

He knew a great deal about life behind the so-called Iron Curtain and hated most of what he knew. But all the same he knew that if his supposition was correct his world was finished. It had no more assets. It had no more time, no more dividends, no more credit. The account was closed and the overdraft finished. There was no alternative.

Ah well, he thought, some people would get used to the change ; most of humanity can adapt themselves to anything. But not him, he was too old a dog to learn new tricks. He was too grounded in one set of values ever to adopt another. He would go out with his world.

But still, it was lunch time, he would at least leave that free from even the thought of shop. He crossed the street and strolled through the crowds to the dim, little-known restaurant which, rain or shine, peace or bombardment, he had visited for the last twenty years.

*

Dr. Hearn was profuse both in thanks and apologies. He pumped Tony's hand and led him like a bridegroom to the waiting taxi.

'My dear boy,' he said, 'I can't tell you how grateful I am to

35

you for helping us out like this. Really most kind. It's too bad that there was nothing to interest us. You know, strictly between ourselves, I do feel that Kirk tends to panic a little. Wonderful man, wonderful career, but perhaps just a little past his prime now. I mean after all, we're not unimportant at Farhill, and he had no right to ask for my best man when the whole business was quite outside our province.'

His plump well-manicured hand opened the door with a flourish, and he handed Tony into the cab as an aged and feeble lady.

'God, what a fool the man is,' thought Tony as they drew away. 'Nothing to interest us, panic a little.'

Although an expert in no subject save his own, surely even a biologist could have some notion of the implications of the meeting. Hearn was disappointed in the fact that at the moment there was no indication that the Russians were cramming their machine full of germ mutations. That was all he cared about.

'All right for you, Hearn, old boy. All right for the dispassionate scientist lying legless in the gutter and still only thinking of his own line of research. But not me, not this child. I care all right.'

The cab crawled and jerked and stopped and crawled on again through central London. The courteous young men on motor bicycles weaving through the traffic, missing pedestrians by inches, but always missing them. Piccadilly and the dark suits from clubs, and the north country crowds huddled miserably round the dripping fountain in the Circus. Soho and the whores already on duty; immeasurably tarnished in the bright sunlight, the old, worn faces showing through the make-up. God in his heaven. Charing Cross Road, with the musty shops of the secondhand booksellers and the long stretch to the Euston Road, where the buses grind all day long through the black streets and the railway arches and the empty theatres. All the way to North London where the wolves seem very close behind the sleigh.

For hours the cab seemed to groan through the traffic, but at long last pulled into the giant copy of a Tsar's riding stable which the directors of the Great Northern Railway had decided should house their terminus.

The Durford train was already waiting. He had time to buy cigarettes and pull himself into the last compartment as it pulled away from the platform.

The *Gadshill* had not made news. None of the papers gave it headlines but merely stated the text of the relayed message. There was too much else of interest it seemed. The divorce of a royal personage, the test match, the forthcoming election. After a time he put them away and leaned back.

Opposite him two pretty women with terrible voices discussed the shopping advantages of Leeds over London. On the seat beside him, two heavy men smoked pipes and talked business.

Near to Peterborough a turkey cock ticket collector took long and suspicious notes of the official pass that Hearn had given him.

The flat east coast scenery rolled by the windows. The pipe smoke spiralled and floated in the thick atmosphere. The north country voices droned on.

He was asleep by the time they reached Durford.

*

Vladimir Ilyich Yakov, formerly gunner's mate in the Imperial Russian Navy, loved children, fat women, and choral music. He sat at the mahogany table in his suite on Manhattan, flanked by his stout wife and two stout daughters, and consumed vast quantities of fish and black coffee.

Behind him a concealed radiogram played recordings of a Cossack choir, and through the window he could see the sun playing on the tower of the Woolworth Building. From every wall of the vast room of gilt and plush, paintings of revolutionary heroes frowned in disapproval of this peaceful bourgeois breakfast.

Vladimir Ilyich was a kindly and peace-loving man. It was long, long ago since he had stood as a boy on the barricades of Tsaritsn and worked his gun till it had jammed with heat. Now he was old and tired and wished to live at peace with everyone.

Although he had utter faith in the cause he served, he hated his work at U.N. and longed for retirement. Then he could live quietly in the Crimea ; his official duties confined to the opening of factories and housing estates and the kissing of shaven, blond children.

As the gilt clock on the mantelpiece struck nine he rose punctually from the table and embracing his wife moved to the door.

He patted the shoulder of the waiter who opened it for him and quickly and pudgily strode down the long heavily carpeted corridor, with a smile and a greeting for all who passed him.

As he entered the office, his good humour left him at the sight of his secretary awaiting him, grim and efficient beside the desk. How he would have liked to have had someone else. A cheery, blonde girl perhaps who would joke with him sometimes. This woman never joked, never even smiled. His breakfast was suddenly sour in his mouth as he looked at the thin, humourless face.

Still the fact remained that he had to put up with her. She was quite indispensable to him. By the time he had trained somebody else to take her place, the work would have gone to pieces. Besides, he was not at all sure how Moscow would take the dismissal of such a loyal and devoted servant of the party. No, Comrade Kniaz was a fixture.

He took his seat behind the huge, ornate desk and began to run through his pile of correspondence.

At the end of half an hour he pushed aside the last document, and put a long brown cigarette to his lips.

'Nothing there,' he thought gratefully, looking at the papers. 'Nothing at all, everything was purely routine.' The conference in the morning would go off exactly as he had planned.

It was strange the British sending out their top man about the sinking of this wretched ship, but it didn't matter. He had his instructions. He would be very polite, very sorry, and deny all knowledge of it. Sir Philip Gloster was a reasonable man, he could talk to Sir Philip. Sir Philip would believe him.

He had always welcomed the new policy of co-operation with the West, and tomorrow he would get up and speak of peace, friendship, and mutual trust. This time he would mean it.

He looked up at his secretary and at once the pleased look on his face was abruptly changed to one of surprise. For she was smiling.

The smile had nothing to do with mirth or humour. There was no friendship or pleasure in her expression, it was merely a drawing back of the lips over the white gums with the eyes remaining as cold as ever. He felt slightly sick as he looked at her smile.

'Well! what is it, Comrade,' he said testily, 'is there anything else for me?'

'Yes, sir,' she said, and it was the first time she had ever called him sir. 'Yes, there is just one other thing, but I didn't want to bother you with it till you had finished your normal mail. There is plenty of time, Comrade Zhakov will not be arriving before two o'clock.'

'Zhakov! what on earth is he coming for?' He felt very worried as he thought of Zhakov. The last of the old guard still holding a vestige of power. The last Stalin extremist, the last of the real unrelenting Bolsheviks.

If Zhakov was at this conference, in any capacity, no progress could be made.

'You should have told me about this at once,' he snapped at the woman, and grabbed the buff paper from her hand.

For a moment his thick, pudgy fingers fumbled with his glasses and then he started to read. But not for very long. Almost at once its meaning was clear to him. He didn't even finish it, there was no need.

He dropped the paper on the desk and leaned back in the heavy, plush chair, and he was no longer a happy, jaunty figure, but an old man who had lived too well. An old man, with bad teeth, a bad heart, a bad digestion. An old man who was out.

The paper in front of him, heavy with seals, made that quite clear. He was out and it was Zhakov who would be representing the Soviet government in the morning. In a few hours the plane would be coming in, and on its arrival he was to become a mere subordinate.

His staff and offices were to be taken over by Zhakov. Zhakov was to address the conference. Zhakov was in complete charge. He was to remain in New York in a purely advisory capacity.

Well, so that was that. The moderates were out and it was the old, implacable extremist who would address Gloster in the morning. He looked up once more as Kniaz spoke to him.

'What was that, Comrade? Oh yes, of course, the arrangements for Comrade Zhakov's reception. I think all the senior staff had better be at the airport to meet him. Would you please see that that is made clear to them. Thank you.'

He rose slowly to his feet and took up one or two papers. Whatever happened he must keep his dignity before this woman. He knew she disliked him, knew how pleased she must be at his fall, it was vital that he kept his dignity.

He might be out, but at least she should never know that he was down. He turned from her and walked quickly and jauntily out of the room.

CHAPTER FIVE

IT was the day before the new session opened and all the week they had been coming to New York.

They walked jauntily off boat and out of aircraft in smoking, gum-chewing groups, and they had come from all over the world. From London they had come and Athens. From Tokyo and Moscow. From Chicago and Paris, France, and they were all quite identical.

They were young and old, short and tall, pink and coffee coloured. They wore light suits, dark suits, neat suits, and disgusting suits. Their ties were as multi-hued as their employers' consciences. Yet they were all the same.

They thought the same thoughts, they dreamed the same dreams, they spoke the same language, they had the same unpleasant ambitions, they carried the same air of tarnished knowledge and superiority. For they were all citizens of one kingdom ; the great kingdom of the press.

All day they congregated in the bars along the East River. It didn't matter which bar so long as it was near the information centre and a phone was always available.

They leaned in groups against the counter, drinking heavily on expenses, or playing cards in the back. Sometimes one of them would move stealthily to the phone booth, and on his return the flow of anecdotes would stop and they would crowd abjectly around him. For occasionally it may be possible to try and swap news ; even with one's bitterest rivals.

They were all the cream of their profession. They were as blasé and cynical as human beings can be, but at the moment they were all very happy and excited, because in the morning, they knew that something was going to break. They didn't know what. The unexpected arrival of the British Foreign Minister was interesting, curious ; but there was still something more.

The subjects on the agenda promised nothing spectacular. This new business of the sunken freighter would take five minutes. Only the atmosphere had changed.

Vague scraps of information had drifted to them from the chatter of waiters and the furtive talk of shabby, bribed men

40

in cafés. Nothing exact. Nothing that added up to anything. Nothing they could possibly write about. But they all pointed to one thing. Something was going to happen in the morning.

The British contingent stood round a bar called 'The Blue Heaven' and waited for Forest. They waited patiently, anxiously, their eyes always turning towards the swing doors, as they swapped smut.

It was three o'clock and they had completely lost him. He had promised to be there at twelve and tell them something and there was still no sign of him. So they waited at the bar and listened for the third time to Nathan's account of the sexual peculiarities of a middle-aged Q.C. and glanced longingly at the door. For Big John Forest was the doyen of his trade.

There was nothing remarkable about him except for his size. He stood six foot three in his socks and his body looked as if it had been rudely carved by a native craftsman. Apart from that he was no different from any of them. He wrote no better copy than they did. He was no more industrious. He had no friends at court. There was no reason why he should be more highly paid, more sought after, more knowledgeable than any of them, except for one thing. He was always there.

He was always there, and that was the reason for success. The thing that mattered. Just being there, in the right place, at the right time.

It had started long, long ago. Long before he was known or successful, before he smoked cigars or wore Savile Row suits. Before he was fat and when he still had knuckles on his hands instead of soft, pink dimples, he had been at just the right place at the right moment.

He had leaned lazily against a dusty wall in a dusty Balkan town, and watched an archduke reel against the fawn cushions of his car as Princeps' bullets tore through him.

That had made him. Very slowly, painstakingly, he had written down what he had seen and then sauntered to Sarajevo post office, to foretell the Great War.

Since then scoop had followed scoop. Never hurrying, never active, never industrious he had drifted round the world, always to the storm centre. So they waited in the bar for him, while the nicotine-ruined voice of Spelman expressed their thoughts.

'The bastard,' said Spelman, 'the fat bastard. He'll have it all by now and be sitting comfortably on his arse, drinking Scotch, and finishing his copy as easy as pie, while we hang about here and wait for him. When he does tell us it'll be as cold as Crippen, and we do nothing.'

'True, Dave, true, what, what can we do? Hawes of the *Sun* was as scraggy as a chicken and his voice was like sand-paper. 'What have we got, Dave? Just tell me that. What have we got that makes us think this conference is going to be different from any other? Yes, that's right, boy. We've got a feeling, a suspicion, that something's up, and John's word for it. Nothing more, or are you hiding something?'

Spelman drained his glass before replying and then leaned back against the bar, looking at his colleagues like a lecturer. 'Yes, I think I've got more than that. Much more, if you're capable of adding up to three. Let me give you three points. Three points that are all unconnected. But I think if you look into them they tell us a little.'

He watched with pleasure as interest lit up their faces. 'Point one. A British tramp steamer reports that she has been rammed by a warship in the White Sea and left sinking,' he said. 'Nothing in that, perhaps, but the Ruski denial comes just a leetle too quickly, don't you think?

'Point two. A certain general, head of a department we are not even allowed to mention, calls on our respected Foreign Minister and four hours later Sir Philip announces that he is coming here in person. Well, I ask you.

'Point three. This same General, the day before he saw the F.S., had called a number of top-line boffins to his office and kept them there most of the afternoon. No, don't ask me how I know, because I don't want to lose my card. But it's true, I promise you. All these may seem to be separate. But I think that if you take—'

'If you take Point four.'

The voice was thick and muddy and seemed to come from far down in the enormous body.

They turned and looked at John Forest walking like a rock from the swinging doors.

'Yes, gentlemen,' he said, 'if you take another point I think you may find that they tie up a little. Thank you, Bill, as always, a double Haig.'

He hoisted himself up on to a creaking stool and the glass looked tiny in his massive hand.

'Point four, gentlemen. The representative of a fairly well-known London journal forgoes the pleasures of his colleagues' company and drags his weary way to the Soviet Embassy. There he sees the usually jovial Yakov looking the picture of misery, leaving with most of his staff.

'He follows them to the airport and watches his excellency, standing like a lackey, as a Soviet plane lands, and a single passenger gets out of it.

42

'I think you will agree that our friend's points do make a little sense when I tell you that the passenger's name was Stephan Zhakov.'

He looked with tolerant amusement as they rushed madly to the phone booths.

*

The motor cycle escort passed explosively and the car drew smoothly up, exactly in the centre of the entrance to the United Nations building.

He came out of the car with a boyish grin and began to walk briskly and confidently up the stairs to the conference hall, pausing for a moment as the press photographers held the bulbs high over their cameras.

'Smile, please, Sir Philip,' they called. And Sir Philip Gloster, Her Britannic Majesty's Foreign Secretary, smiled.

He gave them the smile, the big smile, the smile of patient authority, the suffering, boyish smile that had won him a dozen elections. He bowed politely to the gentlemen of the press, and moved on up the stairs, lightly and easily, his aides behind him.

A man may smile and smile and be a villain, and a man may smile and be afraid. Sir Philip Gloster was afraid.

He was a professional politician and he loved routine. He liked facts neatly stacked and sorted before he considered them. He liked subjects clearly marked and tabulated on the agenda. Subjects which he had checked and considered over and over again. He hated anything out of the ordinary.

The heavy attaché case at his side was full of such subjects. Berlin, the Rhine scheme, customs reforms. He had been through them with his permanent delegate time and time again, and he was familiar with every point on the official list. But this time he knew with utter certainty that the meeting would not be concerned with any of them.

In the last extremity it is the permanent officials, not the politicians, who shape policy, and today it was General Kirk who was giving the orders. Sir Philip was quite resigned to that. He was now a mere agent in the hands of an unpleasant, overbearing fellow in a dusty, over-heated office at the back of Whitehall. The future of Berlin did not matter. The Rhine did not matter. Even this steamer did not matter. All that mattered were Kirk's instructions.

In a few minutes he would get up from his crested chair and talk to the Russians before all the world. He would speak politely at first. He would talk of peace and friendship and other problematic things. Then he would do his job. His lackey's job.

43

He was the heir of a five-hundred-year-old name. The holder of a string of orders like the alphabet, and he knew his duty.

He would throw the loss of the *Gadshill* at the Russians with all the force at his command. He would ask question after question about her loss, and go on asking them, though he had no hope of a satisfactory answer. And all this for one reason only. They might give something away, something that would tell Kirk what they were doing in the restricted area.

As he entered the foyer, he paused and looked round at the crowd slowly filing through into the General Assembly chamber.

He looked for the stocky bulldog figure of Senator Hedges. He wasn't there. That was odd ; he must have gone in already. Usually they talked for a moment and went over last-minute points together. Ah well! Probably Hedges was in the same position as himself. Some grim American General Kirk, as lean as an Indian, would have well primed poor old Hedges. But then Hedges would possibly enjoy it.

Ten generations of politicians in his blood probably made a man a little more wooden and cautious than was desirable. But in any case he knew his duty. He had to hit the Russians with everything that came to hand. With diplomacy, with rudeness, with the kitchen sink, as they said.

The arrival of Zhakov had nearly convinced him that Kirk was right, and if he was right there was nothing to lose anyway.

Ah well, win or lose, Comrade Stephan Zhakov would still have a fight. He would do what he had to do. The British jacks would be thrown down before the Russian aces, and though they achieved nothing, his partner Senator Hedges might still hold a few trumps.

His thoughts hidden from all who saw him, he moved on, light and debonair, into the hall.

As he took his seat he knew that something was wrong. He looked at his slim, gold watch and the time was correct. Before him the Indian delegation sat stolid and unsmiling. His number two was beside him.

But there was something different. Two faces were missing. On the back of every seat was a card bearing the names of the countries represented. The adjoining seats labelled U.S.A. and U.S.S.R. were empty.

Through the plate glass, the press looked down at him as always. The interpreters sat in their little boxes. The pillars winked in summer light, yet his fear was dark.

He rose to his feet and looked round the hall, and then started as the wonderfully calm and aristocratic voice of the president's secretary addressed him.

'Would Your Excellency!' How he hated the term. 'Would Your Excellency be good enough to spare the President a moment of your time, before the conference starts. It really is of the utmost importance. The Russian and American representatives are already with him and they would take it very kindly if you, Sir Philip, would join them.'

He left the hall and followed him out through the curious eyes. They walked down long marble passages, lined with oil paintings, their shoes clicking on the floor. At the end of the building, an attendant held open a door with a flourish, and he walked into the President's chambers.

There were three men who mattered in the room, and Count Hasel, President of the Conference, was not one of them.

He stood by the table and bowed to Sir Philip, and he was very tall, very beautiful, and nothing mattered that he said.

The men who mattered did not speak. True, Senator Hedges winked a red, cynical eye at him as he entered and Yakov smiled and half bowed his fat body. But even these did not matter. The man who mattered did not even turn round.

He stood looking out of the window, the sun playing on the grey, sparse hair of his martyr's head, and he was very still.

The President made his apologies for the interruption. He was sure neither Senator Hedges or Sir Philip would mind, but the Soviet representatives had asked for a private talk before the Session opened. He personally welcomed any more intimate exchanges of ideas. Now he would ask Mr. Zhakov to speak.

The Russian turned from the window, and the eyes were very bright in his tired, old man's face. He was like a lizard on a garden wall, unblinking in the sunlight.

Quite a nice, pleasant old man, one would have thought, A quiet, simple old man in a quiet, simple suit. A nice old man, as long as you didn't look too closely into the eyes ; as long as you didn't think about the Engineers' trial, the liquidation of the Kulaks, the deportations from Poland. As long as you forgot he was Zhakov.

He walked to the table and looked at the thick sheet of paper that Yakov handed to him.

'Here it comes,' thought Sir Philip. 'Here comes the announcement. In a few seconds we will know what they have done in the North. Kirk is too late with his news. We are going to get it from the man in charge. The man who has come to dictate their terms.'

He looked into the grey, bright eyes of Zhakov and waited. For some time the Russian did not speak. He stared at the paper and then opened his hand. The sheet fluttered down on to the floor like an autumn leaf.

He looked puzzledly at it and then lifted a glass of water and put it to his lips. His hand shook as he placed it on the table, and a few drops slopped on the dark, polished wood.

He seemed unable to speak. Twice he opened his mouth, but no words came. He seemed to plead with his audience for help.

And suddenly Sir Philip was no longer afraid. The eyes in front of him were not hostile or triumphant. They were just tired and very, very sad. They seemed about to weep. He was full of hope as he looked into those sad eyes.

And suddenly Zhakov was speaking. His words came in a rush and they were thick and slurred, quite unlike his usually precise English.

'Gentlemen, I must first apologize for keeping you from your business today. I am sure you will forgive me when you have heard what I have to tell you.

'Firstly, Sir Philip, my country now admits that the British steamer *Gadshill* was indeed sunk by a collision with one of our naval units. I am instructed to convey to you our deep regrets, and to say that we accept full responsibility for the loss.'

He paused and ran his hand over his greying head.

'Gentlemen, gentlemen, we have not been good friends in the past, you and I. Our governments have said very hard things to each other, and we have said some very hard personal things. That makes it difficult for me to speak to you now, but I must.

'Gentlemen, I am instructed by my government to ask for your help.

'We ask it not only for the sake of our country, but for the future of the world. Believe me, if you do not grant it there is nothing left for any of us.'

Once more he lifted the glass to his lips and when he spoke again his words were a whisper.

'Gentlemen, a pestilence has broken out in the northern regions of the Soviet Union. A pestilence so terrible that if we cannot stop it we are finished. And so are you.'

He sank back into his chair and for a moment there was silence in the room.

They stood motionless, stunned by his words. Then a soft sound rose and fell around them. Zhakov was sobbing.

CHAPTER SIX

'THE whole thing is quite incredible.'

For the tenth time Hearn said it, and this time his voice had a ring of mania.

'This isn't science, it's madness, mumbo jumbo, the three-headed devil sitting on the ruined church.' No organism can behave, can be made to behave like this.'

He pressed another stub into the already overflowing ash-tray and stared at his colleague.

Tony didn't bother to answer him for a moment. He kept on flicking through the wad of closely typed figures and his face was unshaven and haggard.

'But it has, old boy,' he said slowly. 'It has and does.' The Russian scientists who had drawn up the report had done a fine job, as had the devoted translators and typists. He had every fact dealing with the pestilence on the table before him and not one of them made any sense. He had every necessary clue, and none of them fitted.

He had been studying mutations of one kind or another since he was a boy, but he had never dreamed of anything approaching this. The complete transformation of an organism almost overnight. The change of its growth and habitat. The humble, harmless species becoming the killer.

Almost savagely he pushed the papers away from him and looked at his watch.

'Well, it's almost time now, Kirk said an hour, let's go and see if they are ready for us.'

They pushed back their chairs and went out of the room into the gleaming corridor of the research station. At the end of the passage, outside the lecture hall, Kirk was waiting for them.

Tony's spirits rose slightly as he saw him. Here at least was reality. Somebody completely sane and divorced from the terrible picture imposed by the typescript that he and Hearn had been studying for six hours.

Kirk was probably a scientific ignoramus, but at least he was real, a real person with real wordly common sense. Tony's confidence returned as he looked at him.

The General removed the habitual cigar from his lips and beamed at them.

'Ah, here you are, my dear fellows. I was just coming to fetch you ; they're nearly ready now, I think.'

He led them to the door, talking as he went.

'You know, it's a most unpardonable liberty the F/O putting me in charge like this. Rather like having a bus driver as head of a racing stable, I feel. The general idea appears to be that I am to look after co-ordination and of course security. The last in particular.

'If the herd got to know about this, I needn't tell you what would happen. We'd have riots on our hands which would make the sack of Rome look like a children's outing. That's why, at the moment, you two are completely on your own, apart from collaboration with your opposite numbers in the States, of course. It has rightly or wrongly been decided, here and in Washington, that the thing is to be kept completely in the dark. Even from the medical authorities. You are to work on it with the facilities you have here, and of course—' he looked hard at Hearn—'with any help my department can give you.

'Ah, here we are. Are you gentlemen ready for us?'

The two Russians had flown in that morning, and they were making their final preparations. One of them was working on a cinema projector and the other standing by the screen.

They nodded to Kirk, and waved them to their seats.

'Good, should we start then?' Kirk moved to a switch, and at once the neon lights flicked and the room grew dark.

The Russian by the screen began to talk and his English was clipped and over-correct.

'Good afternoon, gentlemen. I have two exhibits to show you which we hope will give you some idea of what we are up against. The first is a film taken in the area of Purflu and Archangelsk. I am afraid you may find parts of it a little difficult to follow, but I must tell you that the shots were taken in great haste and at great personal risk. The second exhibit I think you may find more instructive.' He snapped his fingers and a white beam waved and fell on the screen.

It was, as he said, difficult to follow. The film was hazy and dark. Sometimes it rose and sank so that often part of the screen was empty.

It showed a tumbledown village, with a row of wooden houses flanking a muddy street. The houses were low and in a terrible state of repair. The paint was peeling from their walls and the roofs sagged. Tony was reminded of an early Western set. In a few minutes a banjo would start to twang from the saloon, a woman would scream, and the killers would come riding into town.

But nobody came. The camera flicked back and forth from house to house and no sign of life appeared.

'Observe now, please, observe the left hand corner of the picture. Observe the house in the corner,' said the Russian. They looked at the corner and the camera seemed to make an effort to steady itself. The house in question looked no different from any of the others. The same low, wooden building, the same chipped façade, the same air of neglect. But yes, it was different, it was moving.

Very slowly in tiny, slow jerky movements, the door was opening. It was incredibly realistic, this slow movement. Tony suddenly felt he was there; far away in the corner of the world, standing in the mud of the deserted street watching the house. Watching the door move open. Listening to the creak of the hinges. Waiting for something to come out.

And suddenly there was something there. Something was revealed in the portal now. Something without shape was standing there. He heard a deep sigh from Hearn, and felt his nails cutting into the palm of his hand. Then the screen suddenly flashed white and the film was ended.

The Russian moved on cat's feet across the room and flicked on the lights.

'Yes, I am sorry, but that was most indistinct. Perhaps you will now please be good enough to come with me. I am sure you will find our second exhibit more useful.'

He led them out of the hall to the small ante-room that stood behind it.

In the back of the room was a huge metal chest, lying on its side, and vaguely reminiscent of an old type travelling trunk. The Russian stood beside it like a showman about to reveal the big act. He did not bow, but you felt he would have liked to.

He bent down and rested his hand on a lever at the side of the case.

'Draw closer, please, gentlemen. There is no danger, there is a glass screen behind the steel. You have nothing to fear. Ah! much better, now you will be able to see.

'What I am going to show you is a specimen of the thing you saw so indistinctly just now.'

He pulled the lever.

The steel top moved back slowly, and as he had said, there was a glass panel behind. The light shone clearly through the glass and lit up the inside of the case and the thing it held.

Tony looked through the glass, and suddenly his head seemed to swell. There was a roaring in his ears and his eyes

were very painful. He gripped the case and forced himself to
go on looking.

So that was it. That was what stood at the end of the maze.
That was the skeleton in the cupboard, the fly in the ointment,
the nigger in the woodpile. That was the thing that ran behind
you in the dream and which you must never see. That was the
Gorgon who turned you to stone.

He turned blindly away from the case, groping for a chair
and fighting his desire to vomit.

*

Hearn's office gleamed with steel and plate glass. He waved
Kirk and Tony to seats of synthetic leather and pulled open a
cupboard.

'I think we can do with some of this,' he said, and placed a
bottle and glasses on the table.

'Too good a brandy to treat lightly, but in the circumstances.' He lifted the half-full tumbler to his mouth and
drained it at a gulp.

Kirk followed suit, and his colour began to improve. 'Ah!
thank you, Doctor, that's much better. Now, gentlemen, we've
seen it. You've been through the available information. What
is it? How does it work? Can we stop it?' His voice was once
more calm and authoritative.

'May I?' Tony glanced at Hearn, and at his nod picked up
the house phone.

'Hullo, is that you, Marsh? Look, it's Heath here. I want
you to go down to the basement, where Mr. Jacobs keeps his
mycelium cultures. Ask him to give you a tray at the fruiting
stage and bring it up here. That's right, to the director's room.
Thank you.'

He put down the phone and turned to Kirk.

'Now, General, when we get these specimens I shall try and
put you in the picture. As far as we are ourselves, that is.
While we're waiting for them, I'll run through the general
history of the disease, as we have it from the Russians. I use
the term disease for want of a better.'

He looked at the thick buff folder and went on.

'Firstly, if you are to understand anything, you have to
realize that what you saw just now could not even loosely
be called a human being. That is absolutely essential. There is
nothing human about it. True it has once been a young woman
of about twenty years of age. It has the remains of arms, legs.
Possibly it even had some form of thought processes before it
was killed. But it could no more be called human than . . .

than that.' He pointed to the rubber plant in the corner of the room.

Kirk nodded. In spite of the brandy, the horror was coming back.

'Good, now let's see how it started. About two months ago the entire population of a fishing village became ill. Not gravely at first. There was some difficulty in breathing and slight internal discomfort. This was followed by a violent fever, which soon cleared up and the patient recovered completely.

'That was in the case of the males. Where women were attacked, the infection spread and you get that.' He waved his hand to the door.

'No woman has died from it, and no woman has been known to have recovered. The female glandular structure seems to be more easily assimilated than the male. As I said, *that* was once a young woman.'

He rubbed his hand across his eyes as if to blot out the horror he had seen.

'Ah thank you, Marsh, put it down there.'

The white-coated assistant placed the tray gently on the table and went out.

'Now, General. This thing is some form of fungoid mutation. What form we do not know. But to give you an idea of what has happened I would like to show you a fungus on a large scale.' He picked up a pencil and pointed to the container.

The tray was filled with rich black compost and the surface dotted with pale, shapely domes.

'These are mushrooms.' He ran his pencil almost lovingly across them.

'But this,' he stirred the compost and revealed a tangle of white threads below the surface. 'This is the mycelium, the creature itself.

'The mushroom, we know, is only the fruiting body, the reproductive device. These are the roots, the branches, the leaves. These threads grow rapidly under the surface, questing everywhere. They have extraordinary powers of penetration for food. Most other organisms make their own food from the atmosphere, or with the aid of light, devour other plants or animals.

'These mushrooms are saprophytes. They live on the dead. The rotting remains of other organisms, of which a fertile soil contains so much.

'Here you see the threads of the mycelium spreading everywhere, invading every cubic inch of territory that can yield them anything, until at last, when it is well established, the

51

creature thrusts up its fruiting bodies to the surface, where they can scatter their spores, and start all over again.'

The pencil moved in his hand and gently split one of the domes, revealing the pinkish gills beneath.

'These are the spores. In certain conditions they may be almost indestructible. There are records of them remaining fertile for over a thousand years. Is that clear so far?'

'Yes, I think so,' said Kirk.

Very slowly his unscientific brain was beginning to understand the relationship between the familiar, loved mushroom and the dreadful thing in the case. Bacon and mushrooms. Toadstools, yellow and musty in a damp wood. White threads in timber, and a carpenter shaking his head and pronouncing dry rot. He became more and more certain that the reality was going to far exceed his worst imaginings.

'Good, then we'll go on. I have shown you these so that you can get some idea of the general working of a fungus.

'Now, you have heard of course of mutations. The change in the habits, and in some cases the actual structure of an organism into a completely different form. This is obviously a mutation of some kind, though far in advance of anything we have yet experienced. Some form of fungus, we don't know which at the moment, has either changed, or more likely been changed into a completely different species.

'With its altered structure and nature it attaches itself to warm-blooded animals. Its spores enter the body by the lungs and establish themselves there. In the case of the lower animals and the human male it appears unable to survive long and soon dies out. In woman it spreads.

'It takes control of the nervous system, absorbing the human cells and blending them with its own molecules. The by-products it produces soon destroy the hormones, the substances that control the balance and life rhythm of the victim, so that you get the terrible physical distortions, the giantism you saw just now. In the last stage, when it has almost assimilated its victim, the fruiting bodies are pushed out through the skin and begin to spread the spores afresh. You saw that too.

'The most dreadful thing about it is this. In no instance does the victim die. Oh yes, the thing you saw was dead, but only because it had been kept in that case and deprived of air. That had killed it. Given normal conditions it would still be alive.'

'Just a minute. You mean alive, in a human sense?'

'Well, hardly human as we mean the word. But as far as the Russians know, the basic human structure is not destroyed. This thing does not kill. It doesn't need to. It is against its interest to kill. It blends its cells with those of the victim, incorporates itself with it.

'In the final form you have a creature that retains a basic human structure and yet its, how shall I put it, its material is purely fungoid. You have a thing that can see and move and very possibly retain some thought processes. Thoughts that if they do exist, will have one aim and one alone. That of spreading itself to others.'

'I see. And a cure, a means of checking it?' Kirk spoke thickly like a drunken man.

'A cure, no chance. No chance at all. Once the spores have established themselves in the system nothing can be done. As for destroying the original organism, possibly. But only if we can get some idea as to the original cause of the mutation. Then we might do something.'

'And you have no idea of what it could be?'

'Idea? I've a hundred ideas and not one of them makes sense. This thing is not natural. It's made. It's been made by a guiding intelligence. It doesn't follow any natural laws, it doesn't work like any normal structure. If I were a miracle worker I might be able to do something. But I'm not. I'm just a poor bloody scientist and I know nothing. God! We've seen what it can do and we sit here and give you a nice little talk on mushrooms. Hearn and I have spent hours over these reports and we know nothing. And all the time, every second we sit here that stuff is spreading.'

He leant forward and buried his face in his hands.

'Take it easy, old boy, just take it easy.' Kirk's voice was very gentle and his hand was on Tony's shoulder. 'Take it easy, we'll make it. We'll lick it all right. Now just tell me this. How quickly does it spread?'

'How quickly? In the body we don't know ; probably about a month from the first stage to the fruiting period. Before that, when the spores are floating in the air, contamination in even a sparsely populated area would be very rapid. Remember these things are minute. Smaller than any similar organisms we have known.'

'I see ; then how long would they float?'

'I don't know, but remember the dust from Krakatoa went round the earth three times.'

'My God,' said Kirk slowly. 'Then the question is, how long have we got?'

'The question now, General,' it was Hearn who spoke. 'The question now is, when will there be an east wind?'

*

Mrs. Baker had had a good day. Every Wednesday was good really, but this had been most successful.

Almost staggering under the weight of her basket, two parcels, and over-heavy coat, she reluctantly left the main street and began to make her way towards the bus station.

It had indeed been a wonderful day when Mr. Baker—she always referred to her husband as Mr. Baker, even to her two married daughters—had thought of Wednesday.

'Stands to reason, Ma,' he had said, 'stands to reason Wednesday's the best day, half day, you see. Everybody's in a rush to get their little bits and pieces together before the shops shut, and you can't expect the young ladies and gentlemen to be so spry on their half day.'

And Mr. Baker had been right. The young ladies and gentlemen thought of the tennis club, the pictures, and the swimming pool, while the last-minute shoppers took their eyes away from the stout, active figure of Mrs. Baker as she rummaged at will through their counters.

Mrs. Baker's cottage was the pride of the village of Holyford. Bright new curtains always adorned the windows and the cupboard shone with china. Her gleaming saucepans were plentiful in the kitchen and three or four packets of detergents always stood on the shelf. Not that in fact she did a great deal of washing, being a firm believer in the American principle that, whenever possible, it is better to replace all soiled or worn-out articles with new. So Wednesdays were most important.

Today everything had gone very smoothly. True she hadn't been able to get young Rob those boots he needed. Nasty sour-looking thing, that ginger-haired bitch in Shepherds. Sometimes she felt like writing to the managers of some of these stores about their assistants. Still, taken by and large, she had done very well. Those nylon nightdresses were lovely and all the socks would come in very handy; terrible one on socks was Mr. Baker.

She rounded the corner and was very pleased to see the little country bus was already waiting.

'Thank you, George,' she said to the grinning conductor 'Yes, give me a hand up with these. Careful with that one though, it's glass. Terrible the price of glass these days.'

She grinned at her fellow passengers, secure in the knowledge that not one article had cost her a penny.

The rickety old bus coughed and spluttered up the hill out of the little market town and meandered through quiet country lanes. It swept past against branches of trees and stopped from time to time by farm gates where cows considered it complacently, and loose-limbed men with sheep dogs climbed aboard.

Mrs. Baker sat in the back and chatted to other stout ladies. They talked about the weather, the prices of things, the strange behaviour of the new vicar, the rudeness of the police-man. It was indeed a very pleasant day, and most successful. Young Rob would just have to wait a little longer for his boots. Perhaps next week that girl would be moved to another counter. They did move them round sometimes.

There was only one fly in the ointment, this wretched tooth-ache. It was really getting nasty. It didn't throb like any toothache she'd ever had but seemed as if the whole side of her face was swelling out. She looked at herself in the cracked mirror opposite her, and yes, there was a large lump.

Still, she'd be all right once she got home. Keep it warm, that was the only way with a toothache. She'd got herself a nice new hot-water bottle on purpose. She could feel it now, tightly wedged against her enormous bosom. She would lie down for a bit when she got home and rest it against her face, that would do the trick.

Certainly she wouldn't dream of sending for old Watson the dentist or Dr. Jacques. Couple of humbugs they were, charg-ing a pound for the first treatment. Besides she and her family had no time for any official figures, medical or otherwise. They kept to themselves and they kept out of trouble, that was their motto.

Susie's baby by that nice, black soldier from America had been a bit of a nuisance, but she had done all right for herself now.

No, there was no need to send for anybody about a silly bit of toothache.

It was bad, though; not so much painful as funny. A kind of tickling as if something was trying to push out of her cheek.

She thought longingly of her bed. The C & A eiderdown, the Boots hot-water bottle, and a nice cup of Lyons tea.

*

It is interesting to know what would have happened if Mrs. Baker had not been a shop lifter and suspicious of the medical authorities. Dr. Jacques and Mr. Watson were not active or very astute men, and it is unlikely that they would have noticed anything strange about her toothache. But if they had noticed something they might have reported it. Then, perhaps it might have reached the right quarters and Tony and Hearn could have acted a little earlier.

55

And if this had happened Mrs. Baker might have lived and at least one child would not continually wake up screaming as he remembered the worst nightmare of them all.

*

'But, darling, don't you see, I haven't a clue, none of us have. This thing isn't normal, it follows no natural laws. The fact that in every case it is only the female that is affected makes it incomprehensible. We don't even know where to begin. Nothing in nature behaves like this. It's got to have been made.'

Tony and Marcia sat on the bed of the little room Hearn had given them at Farhill. They were very close together. Her left hand was in his and with her right she took the cigarette from her mouth and put it between his lips.

'Look, sweet,' she forced herself to appear calm, though she was stunned by his news. 'There's nothing to worry about, because you're going to make it all right. I promise you that, you're going to make it. You say that it is artificial. That means it's made. Well, if somebody can make it, you can check it. I know you, darling, and I've got utter and complete faith in you.'

She watched him inhale deeply, and leaned back on the pillows; she was terribly tired. Tired and sick and ill.

It was less than two hours since she had arrived at Farhill and she was only just beginning to understand the implications of what he had told her.

That morning when Tony had rung her and asked her to join him, she had been terribly happy. She had thrown a few things into a case and rushed to the station, delighted at the thought of seeing him. It was when she was waiting for him in the hall that the first blow had come.

It was the appearance of Hearn that had told her that something was wrong. She had only seen him for a few minutes, but the man was terribly changed. He seemed to have shrunk to half his size and his beautifully cut suit hung on him like sacking. He stammered as he welcomed her, and told her that Tony would be up in a minute, and all the bounce and blatancy had gone out of him.

Then she had seen Tony. He had come walking slowly along the corridor and he looked like a corpse under the neon lights. His face was feverish and haunted and his eyes were too bright. He had clutched her hand, and his own hand was like ice. His voice seemed forced and unnatural. He was very near breakdown.

56

When at last she had him alone in the bedroom, she had gone for him unmercifully.

It was the first time that they had ever had a row, the first time she had ever nagged. But now she had raged and stormed.

After a few minutes he broke down and told her everything. He broke every promise he had made to Kirk. Broke every personal vow to keep it from her and told her. He told her of the restricted area. The fungoid mutation. The obscene thing in the case. The helplessness. He told her every detail he knew.

When he had finished he had broken down and cried like a child in her lap.

*

For a long time they sat on the bed without speaking and then at last he withdrew his hand, put down the cigarette and got up.

'You're right, darling, we'll make it all right. We've got to make it. We've got all the equipment here and the knowledge. All we need is some clue as to the first cause.' He looked at his watch and grinned ruefully. 'One thing we haven't got though is time.' He bent down, kissed her lightly on the forehead and went out.

When she was alone the real horror of the situation came back to her. She knew enough of biology to appreciate the spread of the thing, and enough to know the difficulty of tracing its cause.

But still it would be all right. Tony would find it. He had to for her sake. Somewhere in the bright echoing rooms he was fighting it. The liquids frothing in the tubes, the guinea pigs rattling in the wire cages; and deep down in the basement, the long lines of mushrooms stretching away under the lights.

But when would there be an east wind? Which would come first, Tony's success or the change of the wind? She looked at her face in the glass and tried to picture it as it might be when the wind blew from the east.

And yet there had to be a first cause. What was it he had said? 'Unnaturally formed, as if by a guiding intelligence.' Intelligence, that meant man-made. Formed by human beings.

Could it be the Russians themselves? Could they have done it and let it get out of hand? No, if they had made it they would know the antidote. Not the Russians then, but someone else.

Very far away in the back of her mind something was beginning to stir. Man-made, man-made or—

Somewhere very faintly a bell was beginning to ring. Something she had heard or read or dreamed. A cutting from a paper, a page from a book, a spoken phrase. Man-made or— But this was nonsense. What could she possibly remember that the men below had forgotten? She lay on the bed and closed her eyes, shutting her mind to the unconscious.

It may have been the journey, it may have been the shock of seeing Tony, or the horror of his story. But she was very tired. She lay still on the bed and she slept. And after a time she dreamed.

She dreamed that she was floating gently through the air and coming to Earth. She rested on the ground as light as thistledown and she was standing in a green field. A little beyond her there was a river with lawns and houses stretching down to it, and bright boats on the blue water.

It was a beautiful place and she felt terribly happy. She walked softly across the grass, and there were voices singing in the distance. She turned a corner and the singers were in front of her. A group of children were playing by the bank, singing and dancing together in a ring, their voices clear and sweet in the summer air. She was near enough to recognize the tune now. The old nursery rhyme with the meaningless words.

'A ring a ring o' roses.'

She longed to join them and ran forwards to the whirling circle, her hands outstretched to theirs, as their song came clear and loud. 'A pocket full of posies. A tishoo, a tishoo, we all fall down.'

And yes, they had seen her. The line was spreading out and dancing towards her, circling over the grass and their faces were turning—

She stood rooted to the ground and screamed. She tried to cover her eyes with her hands, to turn and run, but her body was paralysed. She could only stand and stare at the turning faces. The bloated faces, the diseased faces, each ringed with the purple spots of the Black Death. The plague spots. The real ring o' roses.

They were almost on her now, their faces terrible in the sunlight. And then suddenly they were gone. They were gone and she was slowly sinking down through the earth. Down, always down to fall to her knees on a dark wide plain.

After a time she got to her feet and looked around her. There was nothing in sight on the plain, nothing moved, she was quite alone.

But yes, there was something. Very far off at the end of the landscape, something was standing against the sky. She walked towards the shape; she had to, and as she neared it, it began to take form.

It was huge. It towered over the plain and it was dark and tall like a house. But no, not a house. It was far bigger. A mountain. A slender dark mountain, a pillar of stone standing over her.

She stood below it and looked up at the summit of the mountain and it moved. It moved and began to bend down towards her, shutting out the light. It was falling down through the dark sky towards her, as if on hinges. She turned and ran from the falling rock, and even as she ran she heard stones striking the earth around her. She ran and ran, but all the time she knew she was too late. In a minute the stone face would reach her. She could never escape it. The ground heaved under her feet and she lay still on the bed, looking up at the dark shadow cast by the lamp she had neglected to turn off.

With the dream still heavy on her she got up and crossed to the wash basin, turning on the tap and splashing water over her face. As she bent down she suddenly stiffened and peered into the basin.

The plug lay on its side against the white porcelain, black and shiny, glistening in the light. Black and shiny, like the mountain in the dream. The mountain that was going to crush her.

It was coming back now. From far back in her mind something was rushing out. Something that she had to remember. It was not the dream, though the dream was the pointer to it. It was the thing before the dream that was important. The feeling of familiarity that Tony's story had given her. She tried desperately to concentrate. The clue was in the dream, if she could only find it.

And yes, it was coming back. It was something to do with roses that were not roses and a black mountain. A shiny black mountain on a plain. But which mountain? Where was the mountain?

And she had it. It was in Germany, of course. The Black Mountain of Southern Bavaria. But it wasn't the colour that mattered but the material. It was stone that was important. A black stone mountain and roses. Stein for stone and berg for mountain and roses in Germany.

She almost hurled herself across the room and picked up the phone that stood by the bed, the water dripping from her face and leaving little damp blisters on the directory as she dialled a number.

Very quickly a voice answered.

'Hullo, is that the news desk? Is Mr. Forest available, please? Yes, I must speak to him, it's very important.'

Far away at the end of the line, the rich, confident voice of Big John Forest came through to her.

'Hullo, John, it's Marcia Heath here. Look, I want you to try and remember something for me, it's most urgent.'

She asked a question and waited and then for a long time Forest talked. When he had done, she thanked him briefly and then put down the receiver. She thought for a moment and then stepped out of the room and walked down the corridor.

*

Tony and Hearn peered through their masks at the tiny, grey shred under the microscope.

'Yes,' said Hearn, 'it really is very far advanced, isn't it? Even after freezing the cells are still active. Almost complete absorption has been obtained.'

Tony nodded and taking a probe gently placed a drop of clear liquid on the slide. Slowly, hardly perceptibly, the grey shred stirred.

'It still reacts then, even after days of freezing it is still active. It would be, of course, because even if it has absorbed the human tissue it keeps its own structure and entity. Oh Hell! What's that?'

There was a knock on the door, and with a gesture of impatience he got up from the instrument and opened it.

'Well, what is it, Smith? I thought we told you we weren't to be disturbed on any account whatsoever.'

The porter was red-faced and very embarrassed. 'Beg pardon, sir. I'm very sorry, sir, but it's your wife, Mrs. Heath, sir. 'Ighly important she said it was. She's waiting outside now, sir.'

'Oh, very well then. Hold on for a moment, Hearn, I won't be long.'

He crossed the lobby and went through into the corridor where Marcia was waiting.

'Darling, honestly, you musn't come here. We've given orders that this part of the building is forbidden to all female staff. As far as we know the stuff is still active.'

'Yes, Tony, I'm sorry, but I think this may be important. Just now when we were talking upstairs you said it seemed as if there was an intelligent cause, a directing force. Well, Tony, don't you remember, don't you remember Steinberg, Rosa Steinberg, Tony?'

She watched his eyes light up with comprehension behind the mask, and then started as a voice spoke at her side.

'Well, well, young lady. You could be right at that,' said Kirk. 'You just could be right. You've got a smart wife here, boy, very smart. Nineteen forty-five, eh, my dear. Nineteen forty-five, Ruhleben camp, and Fräulein Rosa Steinberg.'

CHAPTER SEVEN

By the spring of forty-three, only the insane thought that Germany could still win the war by orthodox methods. Stalingrad and Alamein had been fought and lost. The last major U-boat campaign had dwindled to nothing and the Yellow tide in the east was on the ebb.

The insane sat in the shelters of their burning cities, calling up non-existent reserves and moving imaginary armies. They spoke of heroism, of the teutonic gods, of further sacrifice. And nothing they said or did mattered at all. It was with the half-sane that the future belonged.

The half-sane thought of new, and sometimes mystical methods of warfare. They worked on the Schnorkel devices for submarines which would drive the allied convoys off the sea. They planned jet aeroplanes and dreamed all the time of the V weapons that would soon be in production.

With their help, the old enemy across the channel would be brought to her knees, the tired armies in the east would go forward again and the Japanese would stand on the American coastline.

All this they thought, and suddenly it was just a dream. The Norwegians blasted the heavy water tanks, the bombers found the research station at Peenemunde, and it was all too late. They would have to start again, start with other technicians, and there was no time.

After that the mystical weapons came forward. They studied the stars and Norse runes. They sat with soothsayers and dreamed of Götterdämmerung and the end of the world. The end of the world, or the day when a hand would reach for their shoulder and the time had come to crunch the cyanide. That was the time of despair for most of the half-sane. But for one of them, a Kreisleiter of a small northern province, it was the beginning of hope.

He was nobody of importance. When a few months later he was killed in a bombing raid there was no sorrow in Berlin or joy in London. His death made no impact on the course of history. There was only one thing of interest about him. Once he had adopted a child.

It was in the early days of the Party. The days of the noisy meetings in little provincial towns and the back streets of cities. The days of the groups huddled in the smoke of the beer cellars, and the sudden flash of knives in the underground stations. The days of contempt.

He had been speaking in a market town in Silesia. It was a quiet meeting with little hostility, and no enthusiasm except from his own known supporters. The country audience had not been badly hit by the depression and were mainly indifferent. Except for one of them, however. In the far corner of the square, at the edge of the crowd and the lights, a girl was standing. A light fair-haired girl, her body looking about ten, but her face the face of an old woman.

All through the meeting she stood and stared at him, her eyes bright in the glow of the torches as she looked at the stiff flags, and the tall figures on the platform, and the little pudgy man who spoke of blood and land and a new hope for Germany.

When at last the meeting broke up she still waited, watching him. He asked his local colleagues who she was but they were all completely indifferent. She was a vagabond, they supposed. Germany was full of such cases since the betrayal. There was some story about her, the father was said to have been executed for murder and the mother had left her, but it was of no importance. How did she live? They had no idea. A little begging, a little stealing probably, sleeping where she could, half-witted possibly. The matter was completely trivial. In any case, the Mayor was expecting them to dinner, it would not do to be late.

That night he could not sleep. He tossed in the blankets and looked about the room, and from every corner of the plush hotel bedroom the bright, pleading eyes seemed to be looking at him. At about two he couldn't stand it any longer, but got up and dressed. He summoned a grumbling, sleepy porter and together they went out.

After an hour's search they found her. She was crouched in the corner of a disused cellar that stank of rats and decay, surrounded by scraps raided from the dustbins. She had glowered at him at first and drawn back into the darkness, like a small frightened animal, and then allowed herself to be taken away.

Back at the hotel he had washed her with his own hands and cut off most of her bedraggled hair. Then he had dressed her

in a suit of his pyjamas and sat her down before the bedroom fire and they had talked.

They talked for hours, right through to the sunrise and the maid coming in with the coffee ; and by that time he knew that he had no twelve-year-old half-wit on his hands, but a genius. He had taken her home with him that morning. Home through the pitying smiles of his supporters and the hotel staff, to his town in the north. There he had legally adopted her and she became known as Rosa Steinberg.

Very soon he knew that his first impression was right. She was brilliant. Although her slight body developed very little, her mind seemed to grow each day.

He sent her to the local school, and every term when the exams came round there was the name Steinberg at the top of the list. She made no friends. She sat sullen and alone in her desk, answering questions in quiet monosyllables, disliked by both staff and pupils. Her only object of affection appeared to be himself.

He remembered how the headmistress had called to see him one day. She had been most complimentary at first. Rosa's attainments were excellent. Never had the school had such a brilliant pupil. It was a great honour to teach her. There was one thing that she felt she should mention, however. Rosa was too withdrawn. She had been at the school now for over two years, and not once had she been seen playing with the other children. She couldn't remember an instance when she had been known to smile. It was very worrying. Although the mind was developing, the social senses seemed completely dead. The latest advances in psychology pointed out—

That had done it. The term psychology was enough for him. An invention of Jewish bandits, decadents, human filth. What the country needed was minds who could work for the Reich and the leader, not coddled scientific freaks. He had shown her roughly to the door.

When Rosa left school he sent her to Berlin and Munich studying physics and biology. She worked feverishly night and day through term and holidays and took the highest possible degrees.

He was terribly proud of her. The rebuilding of the Reich called for scientists of ability and she would be his gift to the Fatherland. But he was disappointed ; Rosa did nothing.

Once she had finished her studies she came home and did nothing at all. She fitted out a little room at the back of the flat as an office and laboratory and spent her time there. He saw very little of her. The war came and with it the increase of his duties and he was rarely at home. When he did see her

63

he tried to plead with her, to even force her to take up responsible work, but it was no use. Always the bright stare of her eyes silenced him and he left her alone. Poring over her books and formulae, year after year.

One night, towards the end of forty-three, when he had been inspecting some anti-aircraft defences in the area, he came home late and found her waiting for him in the hall. He had been out all day and he still had his report to write. He kissed her perfunctorily and went into his office.

She followed him through and laid a thick folder on the desk.

'Papa.' She had always called him that. 'Papa, you know how you have always wanted to see me working for the Reich.'

He was very tired and he hardly heard her. 'Yes, yes, my dear, but I don't want to force you. I know what you feel about it.'

'No, Papa, I do not think you understand, you have never understood. I did not want to go to work until I could offer something of value. Well, now I can. Now at last I am ready.'

He was delighted. He got up from his chair, his tiredness gone, and poured himself a glass of schnapps as a celebration, thinking how many old friends in ministries he could call on to find her a responsible post.

'Ah, Rosa, excellent, excellent, my child. Tomorrow we'll see what department can take you in.' He gripped her thin arm in his pleasure.

'No, Papa, you still do not understand, do you? I do not want any petty job in a department. I want my own department.'

'Your own department? But this is ridiculous! perhaps in time, but now! I don't know what you mean.'

'You will, Papa, you will. Just read those papers I have put on the desk. I've made them as non-technical as I can, and I think you will understand.'

She got up and went out of the room.

He picked up the papers, half irritated and half curious. Then, warmed by the drink, he began to read. He read slowly, for though she had said it was as non-technical as possible, it was still difficult for the layman. He read for hours and at last comprehension began, and with comprehension he suddenly felt sick and cold.

So! This was what he had fostered all these years. This was the climax to the years at Berlin and Munich. The days in the backroom. Well, it was natural, probably. The raided dustbins, the rat-ridden cellar, and the tainted parency were bearing fruit.

He took up the papers in his hand and walked across the room. There could be only one place for them. He opened the door of the stove and peered inside. A few embers were still glowing. And suddenly he paused and looked up.

On the wall behind the stove there hung a big map of the world. How large it looked, and how tiny was the outline of Germany. He stared at the huge domains of his country's enemies and very slowly his hand fell to his side. No, the decision was not his. He had no right to weigh his own conscience with the fate of his torn, encircled country. Whatever was decided must come from above.

The next day he left for Berlin.

The city was not as he remembered it. Already the rubble was high in the streets and even the outline was beginning to change. Everything was like a nightmare. He called on old comrades and friends, and though they were polite, they were indifferent to him. He could see nobody in authority. For hours he waited in ante-rooms and knocked on the bronze-studded doors of Ministries. But it was no good, nobody wanted him.

He was almost on the point of leaving for home when the summons came, and he was ordered to an address in the Wilhelmstrasse.

He hurried through the rubble in a decrepit taxi and got out at an enormous white building. He walked across a gleaming hall of black and gold, and was borne upwards in a lift like a fairy-tale coach. He crossed marble passages flanked by still, uniformed figures, and at last was bowed through an ante-room like a station into a small, dingy office, as bare and drab as a hermit's cell.

There was a white, deal desk in the room and a little man sat behind it. He got up politely as Steinberg entered and waved him to a seat. He had a weak chin and pale, watery eyes, and he was as mild and obsequious as a minor government official.

'It is very good of you to come so promptly to see me, Herr Untergruppenführer,' he said. 'Very good. I wanted to speak to you personally about these papers you deposited with the Speer Organization. They are not, of course, the real or proper concern of my department, but one of the officials there thought I ought to see them. Yes, he thought so.'

He put on a pair of spectacles and peered at them short-sightedly for a moment, then pushed them aside and stood up.

'They have been rejected, of course, you know that, Herr

C

Steinberg, don't you? They have been rejected on the grounds of inhumanity.' He looked hard at him as he spoke, and he was no longer mild, but a tiger.

'They have been rejected because there are soft men in Germany. Who are the two people who are completely in charge of all military research today? Speer and Goering, I think. Speer and Goering. Incompetent, pleasure loving, weak. Traitors.' He spat the words.

'They have categorically refused this on the grounds of inhumanity, at a time our country is literally being torn to pieces, from both ends. But I! I would use everything in my power to end this war even if I made the name of Germany stink in the nostrils of the world for a thousand years.' He paused and sat down. He was once more mild and distant.

'But then you see I haven't the power at the moment. It is unfortunately not my department, not my concern. Tell your daughter that. Thank her for her efforts. But tell her I can do nothing. Nothing yet. And now good-day, Herr Untergruppen-führer.'

When he was left alone, the little man wiped his forehead with a handkerchief and put a small white tablet to his lips. He gazed at the papers for a moment and then opened a drawer and took out a leather-bound book. It was a collection of Norse legends and he read it with love and care. For Heinrich Himmler was very fond of fairy tales.

Rosa took the news of the rejection calmly, almost indifferently. 'Don't worry, Papa,' she said, 'they'll want it. They'll want it and very soon. They'll have to want it whether they like it or not.'

She was right. The winter drew to its disastrous end. The news got worse and worse. Peenemunde was destroyed and another star rose over Speer and Goering, and the new star remembered a woman called Rosa Steinberg.

One day a fleet of cars drew up in the town completely unannounced. Guards poured out of them and surrounded the block of flats, and amid bowings and scrapings from the local officials, hurriedly congregating in the square, a small, uncertain, childish figure walked up the steps.

Himmler placed his cap carefully on the table and waved his subordinates out of the room. Then he put on his glasses and looked hard at Rosa. He was terribly disappointed at what he saw.

Was this what he had driven all the way from Berlin to see? This childish creature. He had expected some capable woman. Steady and strong and already middle-aged, who would at once give him a feeling of security. That, or better still, some-

one of his own kind. Some mystic, dreaming of occult forces fighting for the Fatherland.

But this! He eyed the tiny, almost stunted body, the pale face and lank hair. The dusty woollen cardigan, already beginning to unravel. This was ridiculous. What could this creature do that the best scientific brains of the country, of Europe, were unable to? His advisers had frowned on the project. Even if it were possible, they had told him, the dangers were too great.

And yet there was seomething. Something of power in her expression. He looked into the pale unflinching stare of those bright eyes and turned away his face.

'Well, Fräulein,' he said, staring out of the window, his back towards her. 'Some time ago the Speer Ministerium passed on to me a scheme of yours that you thought might be of service to us. I read this project with interest. At the time it was considered quite inopportune to apply it. Now the situation has changed.

Behind the words lay the reality of the change. The crumbling cities, the broken front in the East, the French bridgeheads, and above all the blackened ruins of Peenemunde and the dead scientists who lay beneath them.

'And so, Fräulein,' he turned and drew himself up to his full height, 'and so your Reichsführer has come to see you.' This was where the clarion call speech should have come. The call to duty, the need for unsparing efforts in the service of the leader. The honour he was doing to a simple German girl. But none of it came. Under the stare of those cold eyes nothing came. He threw himself down in a chair, the sunlight winking on his polished boots, and spoke quietly.

'But will it work, Fräulein, will it work? If I give you the facilities you ask for, can you be sure it will work? My advisers tell me it will not.'

'It will work, Herr Himmler.' Only his intimates dared to call him by his name, without title or respect. 'It will work; but how long have I got? If you had come to me months ago when my father went to Berlin, it would have been easy. But now, how much longer have I got before every inch of this country is overrun by the enemy?'

'Fräulein Steinberg, I forbid you to speak in that manner.' He was on familiar ground now. 'Last week I sentenced ten people to death for defeatism, no worse than what you have just spoken. Our victory is not in doubt, it never has been. I am merely looking for a means to shorten the war and ease the strain on our people.'

She laughed in his face and her laugh was not pleasant.

67

'Then you do not really need me, do you, Herr Himmler? I assure you that the methods I recommend are too drastic to use if you have others at your command. But tell me this, those ten people you shot. How many Russian tanks were destroyed by their death? How many American bombers came down when they died? No, Herr Reichminister Himmler; I shall speak as I like, and you will do nothing to stop me, because I am the last card you have left. The last cock in the basket.

'I agree with you in one thing, though. Our final victory is not in doubt. It never can be while I hold this in my head.' She pointed to the papers on the table before her.

For a time the little man did not answer. He took off his glasses and polished them, peering short-sightedly at the lenses, and armies marched behind his eyes.

'Very well, Fräulein,' he said at last, 'how much time do you need?'

'How much time? I cannot say exactly. Although all the basic data are now worked out, you must understand that we are dealing with plant and animal structures which are not constant in the time factor. I should say that at the very earliest the spores could be ready in twelve months and at the worst eighteen. The actual dissemination is of course no concern of mine.'

'I see.' He leaned back in his chair and thought for a moment. She was right, there was very little hope left. He had to try everything. The woman was probably insane, but her work might be what she claimed. 'Very well, you can go ahead. Let me have a list of what equipment, experimental subjects, and assistants you need and I shall see that you get them. I shall arrange that buildings at Ruhleben are handed over to you. It is better that you are in an uninhabited area. That is all, Fräulein.'

He rose to go and picked up his hat from the table, and then paused. 'Well, is there anything else you have to say to me?'

'Yes, there is just one little point I think you should know. When you asked me just now if it would work, I told you there was no doubt about it. That is true. Let the allies be held back for eighteen months and the matter is finished. That I promise you. The trouble is that it may work too well. At the moment I am afraid that there is no certain way of stopping the spread of the spores once they are released. I am working on it now, but if I do not succeed, it could be Germany as well as the rest of the world that died. But do not worry, I will find a way. There is no danger. I will find a way, given time.

Oh, but I'm sorry, I forgot. You have no time, have you, Herr Reichminister?'

Once more, Heinrich Himmler, the most feared and hated man in the world, drew back from that terrible smile.

CHAPTER EIGHT

KIRK thanked the sergeant and dismissed him with a nod. He didn't bother to look at the papers, but turned to Hearn and Tony.

'Well, that's it, gentlemen, that's everything the War Office have on the camp and little Miss Steinberg. In a minute I'll hand round the copies and we'll go through them ; but first I want your preliminary opinions on the possibility of all this tying up.' He looked at Marcia.

'You, my dear, have very cleverly remembered the story of a German research station we captured in March forty-five, in which it was rumoured that they were experimenting with fungoid mutations, and using human subjects for these experiments. I use the word rumoured, because I remember there was hardly any definite information to go on. The Germans destroyed so much of the equipment that it was virtually impossible to form any real opinion as to what they were actually after, and three members of the staff we got hold of gave away very little.

'Now, Doctor, when Heath was describing the workings of, of that—' he looked at the door at his side. 'I was struck by his use of the term intelligence. He seemed to imply that it had in some way been directed to behave in its present manner. What I want to know is this. Do you think there may be the possibility of a link-up with our present problem and this German business, or are we merely wasting time considering it?'

Hearn looked up from the table and grinned ruefully at him. 'You know, sir, that's a question I would like notice of. Without committing myself, I should say there was a possibility, but very little probability. So many things are possible, after all. A great deal of our civilization is built upon mutations of one form or another. The whole theory of germ warfare depends on them.

'You see, General, every living thing is in a sense a potential killer. Often the attack is repulsed, because the victim has built up enough protective devices of its own. But change a species, change it so that it chooses a new form of victim, selects something that it has never associated itself with, and which has no defence against it, and you get a killer. The Black Death, for example, the Irish potato blight, the parrot disease scare between the wars, and possibly this.

'Now all this is very possible. The Germans may have been working on some kind of fungoid mutation, but it seems unlikely ; there would have been so much danger to their own people. Besides it is all long ago, and you yourself said that there was very little evidence to hand.

'No, with all due respect to Mrs. Heath and yourself, I personally consider that this is a waste of time, and time is the one thing we haven't got. Our job is with what we know. We have specimens, equipment, we are in close contact with the Americans and the Russians. We have all the necessary data to hand. If we attack this thing by proper scientific methods. Take it to pieces, find out its basic structure, how it reacts to certain stimulants, what are its radiations. When we have that we may find its first cause and do something about it.'

'One moment, old man.' Tony's voice was very gentle, but his eyes were hard. 'You say that we must use proper scientific methods, orthodox methods. Good, excellent. I agree with you that we have all the data we need, that in time we will find a means to destroy it. But how much time, and how long have we got? Why, before we even begin to grasp the cause of this creature's change we would be too late. We know from these,' he tapped the Russian papers, 'the rate of infection once the spores reach the lung tissues. We know the period of incubation in the blood stream. Four to five weeks with the patient feeling only slight inconvenience after the first fever has passed.

'How long, I ask you, before we begin to understand anything at all? We would have to study hundreds of cases from the first spread of the spores to the final absorption of the human cells. God! if that thing in there had been alive it wouldn't have even begun to reach its final form. It would take us months, and we haven't got months, we haven't even got days. All we've got is this straw about Steinberg. Oh, I suppose we could do it. We could make this place air-tight and keep only the male staff. We could take it slowly to bits, test its radiations, and at last walk out with a nice safe inoculation. But what would we find to inoculate? I don't think there would be anything left, you know. I think we would find a fungoid world.'

'You both seem to feel that there is enough in that report you have just read to give a strong case for presuming that the mutation you have described, and which we have seen, is the same thing that they were working on at Ruhleben camp. Fair enough, you are probably right. In any case I think we ought to assume so. That leaves our way clear. Your job is to find out everything you can about that thing in there, as Dr. Hearn said. And mine, well, I think I'd better find Miss Steinberg.'

Tony was suddenly struck by the change in Kirk. A few moments ago he had seemed to be still crushed and bewildered by what he had seen ; now there was something buoyant and confident about him.

'But, General,' he said, 'all that was years ago. If they couldn't find her then, at the time, how can you hope to now!'

Kirk grinned at him. 'Each to his trade, my boy, each to his trade. When you were talking just now, I felt all the time how very unwise it was for my masters to have put me in charge of this business. Your scientific jargon meant nothing to me. I felt completely useless. All that rang a bell for me was this good lady's mention of a name.

'Names are my trade, you know, remembering little forgotten facts is my trade, finding people is my trade, tracing the career of Fräulein Steinberg and her associates is my trade. At last I'm back on a job I thoroughly understand—but what is it, my boy, what are you staring at?'

'I'm not sure yet, sir, but may I have those papers a moment, yes, the last sheet.' Tony leaned across the table and took it. 'Ah, I thought so, the signature, I knew I'd seen that signature somewhere before. Of course. Captain Roberts, Captain A. R. Roberts, now Professor A. R. Roberts, my immediate superior at Durford.'

The General did not seem particularly interested.

'Really,' he said, 'you mean to tell me that this wretched, incompetent fellow, Captain Roberts, has been made a Professor ; extraordinary thing. Well, I suppose it helps us in a way. We would have to have seen him in any case, and as you know him, it should make it easier.

'Now we know where we are! You are in this now, my dear,' he smiled at Marcia. 'When I heard that your husband had disobeyed my instructions and told you about this business, I was most annoyed. Now I feel like blessing him. If we have any hope at all, that hope comes from you.

'Very well, this is what we shall do. You, Doctor, you will stay here. I needn't tell you what line to take, but even if Heath is right and there is no possible antidote, or whatever

73

you call it, that can be ready in time, you must do all you can by analytical methods. Keep in touch with our American friends.

'I want you, Heath, to take your wife as your assistant and go to Durford. See this Roberts. Don't tell him why you want to know, but make him go through everything he remembers about the camp. Everything. Doesn't matter how trivial it seems, I want everything he knows. Any further details as to the place itself, any chance remarks Steinberg or her associates may have made. Anything at all.

'I'll go back to my office and start my wheels turning there. As we have decided that Steinberg is the centre of our circle, I had better start near Ruhleben. It's not far from Hamburg and I have many friends in Hamburg. Yes, I'll send a man to Hamburg tonight. As you said, Doctor, it's a long time ago. A lot of water will have gone past and Rosa and her associates will have gone too. Yet if any of them are still alive, my friends will find them.'

He pushed back his chair and stood up. 'Well, we've not much time, so let's get going. It's going to be a long chase, but with a bit of luck we'll beat this thing. So let's wish ourselves luck, all the luck in the world.'

He held out his twisted hand and motioned them to the door.

*

Mrs. Baker lay in her comfortable bed and she kept still. It was important to keep still. Just keep still, lie quietly and not be bothered.

Outside the door she could hear her family. They knocked on the door from time to time and asked her if she wanted anything.

Why couldn't they leave her alone? How many times did she have to tell them to leave her alone! All she wanted to do was to be left alone.

To lie quietly quite alone and let things take their course. That was what she wanted, what she had to do.

She was in no pain. She was quite all right. It was rather a pleasant sensation really. Like growing something. Like a painless birth. Before long she would be able to get up and go out and walk in the wind with what she had grown.

But not now, not yet. All she had to do now was to lie on her bed, see no one, and keep still—keep still—keep still—

CHAPTER NINE

THE big car that Kirk had lent them didn't talk about its work, but it came down the road like a tornado.

Most of the time the speedometer hung motionless just under the maximum register, sinking occasionally like an arm when the headlights picked up the long lines of lorries and trailers grinding their weary way to the North. Then the foot came down again on the pedal and silent, except for the scream of the tyres, they tore on through the night.

Dawn was already beginning to break. Over the rolling contours of Yorkshire, thin, grey streaks had started to invade the darkness. The trees and hedges no longer looked like tunnels in the light but took on their own vaguer contours.

At last Marcia switched off the lights and looked at Tony stretched out beside her. Much against his will she had insisted on driving, and on his getting at least a little sleep. He had grumbled at first and then, his head half on the cushions and half against her shoulder, he had gone off like a child.

She looked at the clock and began to slow down. It was just after five, and they couldn't be too early. Her body felt sticky with sweat under her clothes. It was not heat or the exertion of driving. The big car was beautifully ventilated and almost drove itself. It was fear. Fear had been behind her all the way from London. The feeling that all that mattered in the Universe was the rise and fall of the speedometer. Every road junction, every lorry that had pulled back that steel arm was somehow her enemy, put in her path to stop her so that the thing behind them could slowly gain ground.

It had nothing to do with reality. She knew the need for speed, the need to find out any detail that Roberts might remember, but this was purely neurotic. It had nothing to do with the job in hand, nothing to do with getting quickly to Roberts. She dreaded the thought of Roberts and that gaunt, bleak house.

What she wanted was to get home. Home with Tony. Home and bar and seal every window and door in the house against the creature in the case. Then there would just be herself and Tony, shut in and away from it, and she could go upstairs and undress and get into a bath. She would lie in it for hours. Soaking in it, wallowing in it, till at last she had washed away everything she had seen and heard at Farhill.

With the light coming up over the soft country she began to feel sane again. They had come a hundred and seventy miles in three hours, they could relax a minute.

She slowed down and, swinging the car on to the low verge, switched off the engine and leaned back.

Soon she felt Tony stirring at her side. He yawned deeply, ran his hands through his hair and then was quite awake. He looked up and smiled at her.

'Where are we, darling?'

'I'm not sure exactly, but we must be almost there, about another five or ten miles to Durford, I should think.'

'Good girl, you've done very well, haven't you?' He glanced at the clock. 'Phew, how many people did you kill?'

'Oh, not many, two blind men and a child. One of the blind men may have got away.'

In the rising light they could still feebly joke.

'Tony,' she picked up his hand and played with the fingers. 'Darling, you don't think that Hearn was right at first, do you?'

'Hearn right about what?'

'What he said at the beginning, that you, that is we, may be wasting our time. That this is all a wild goose chase. That it is so long ago. I mean Roberts seems such a silly, vague old man. Do you really think he will remember anything, after all these years, that he ever knew anything which could help?'

'I don't know, sweet, I just don't know. But we've got to try. What I said to Kirk was quite correct. We've no time to work with normal methods. This Steinberg business has got to be the answer, it's got to be.' She winced as his fingers clenched round her hand.

'Besides, I don't know about Roberts; under that foolishness, I think he has quite a good mind. He must remember something. He's got to remember something that will give Kirk a lead. Anyway, let's pray that he does.

'Come on, my sweet, let's go. I'll take her now.'

He half lifted her and half slid under her and took his place by the wheel. He let in the smooth clutch, almost fiercely. The wheels spun for a moment on the grass, caught, and spun again and then they were off.

It was not far; after about ten minutes, the road forked sharply to the right and they began to climb. At the top of the hill the ground dropped abruptly away and at the end of the valley, perched high on the hill, its slag heaps, factories, and scars still screened by the thin light, only the cathedral clear and wonderful, was Durford. Ignoring the view, Tony drove fast down the slope and through the valley. They crossed the bridge and slowed down in the maze of mean streets at the foot of the hill.

Marcia leaned forward, watching the road signs to direct him, and was struck by the change in the atmosphere that the early morning gave it.

Without the crowds, the weeping children, and the garish lights of the pubs and the tripe shops the area was almost pleasant. There was a freshness about it. The dull river seemed sparkling, and the painted funnels of the ships were gay and romantic. It was as if the night air had washed out all the traces of murky humanity. The houses were still shabby and worn, but the air of decay was missing ; even the Professor's tall house was no longer menacing.

She got out of the car before the ill-kept garden and looked around her, thankful for the clean air and the absence of a crowd of urchins fingering the chrome and enamel.

'Well,' said Tony as he came to her side. 'It certainly isn't much of a place, is it? I suppose we'd better get it over with. He's not going to like one of his assistants knocking him up at this hour and asking him a lot of questions he's probably forgotten about, but it's got to be done. Come on.'

He walked through the gate and across the weed-grown garden and pulled the rusty handle. Once more she heard the far-off bell sound in the murky back regions.

Even the most trivial things come as a shock when completely unexpected. They stood before the door, thinking that it would be hours before they could wake anybody, before Roberts would begin to be aware of the bell, when it opened. Tony's hand had scarcely left the handle when the bolt slid back, the door creaked open, and the Professor, fully dressed, stood before them.

'Good heavens! It's you, Heath, and your wife, what on earth! No, no,' he waved aside Tony's apologies. 'The time doesn't matter at all. As you can see I was up. Sometimes I can't sleep, you know, and then I get dressed and try to work. I heard a car and wondered who it could be.

'But you, what on earth do you want at this hour of the morning?' He stood in the doorway, making no sign for them to enter.

'I'm sorry, sir, very sorry,' said Tony. 'I know how odd this must seem, but the fact is I have to talk to you. I've just come down from Farhill on government instructions. It's very important, sir, please let us in.'

'Come in, of course, come in. But talk to me? Government

instructions, this hour. Very strange. But still, if you must, you must.'

He turned sharply on his heel and shuffled across the hall, motioning them to follow him.

As they walked after him, Marcia was once more struck by the thick smell of incense. It hung over everything, terribly strong and stupefying after the morning air. She paused for a moment and felt Tony stop at her side. Then the querulous voice of Roberts hurried them on into the drawing-room.

He motioned them into chairs, but himself remained standing. 'Well now, what is it, Mr. Heath, what can I do for you? As I have said, there was no question of getting me out of bed, but all the same I do find your calling on me at this hour a little odd. Odd, and I'm afraid I must say, a little distasteful.'

'I quite realize that, Professor,' said Tony, 'and as I just said, I'm sorry about the time, but I do assure you that it is most vital that I ask you one or two questions. And ask them now.'

'Questions, what questions, you talk like a policeman. Let's get down to these questions.'

'Very well, Professor.' Tony opened his case and took out some sheets of paper. 'Perhaps you'd look at these and see if you can recognize them.'

Roberts fumbled in his worn pocket and pulled out a gold pincenez. He adjusted it carefully on his nose and then sat down and looked at the papers. He only read for a few lines and then he stopped. His breathing seemed to grow quicker. His face flushed and suddenly his fingers opened and the sheets fluttered on the floor around him.

'Oh, I'm sorry, I don't know what came over me. It's like seeing a ghost.' He scrambled on the floor, retrieving the papers.

'Yes, of course I recognize this. It's the report I wrote on a German research camp we captured in forty-five. But what about it? What do you want to know about it? Why do you question it, what has it to do with you?'

'I can't tell you, Professor. You must take my word for it. You'll have official confirmation before long, but at the moment I can't tell you anything except that the Foreign Office are very interested in this camp and want a little more information on it.

'This report you wrote, now. There are one or two points which are not too clear. I want you to explain them.'

'I see. I knew, of course, that you had been allowed leave of absence for some official business, but this, this report is years old. I thought it was all forgotten and passed over. What is it, Heath, why do they suddenly try and dig it up?'

Marcia watched Tony slowly shake his head and then looked at Roberts. His expression had completely changed. At first he had seemed merely surprised and irritated at their visit. Then he had been curious, but now there was something else in his face. Yes, he was proud. His lined face looked at Tony, but his eyes kept glancing down to the papers on the desk, and there was pride and satisfaction in them.

'Once more, sorry, Professor,' said Tony. 'I can't tell you a thing. I'd personally like to, but my orders are quite definite about it.'

He leaned forward and took up the report.

'Now, Professor, on these pages you give a description of the lay-out of the camp. It is very brief, isn't it? I know of course that you had very little time there and the Germans had almost completely destroyed the equipment, but I want you to try and remember any further details you haven't put here. Anything at all, it doesn't matter how trivial they seemed at the time.'

'Oh, I see. I see it all now. I see why they've sent you, Heath.' The grey face was taking on a slight flush.

'Well, so they're at last interested in Steinberg, are they? After all these years they're interested. I could have saved them a lot of bother, if they'd have listened to me, you know. I told them at the time. As soon as I saw that camp I knew that something horrible had been going on there. I got through to H.Q. and told them a thorough examination was needed, that it was essential in fact, but they only laughed at me. Natural I suppose. There was a lot going on at the time and brass hats don't like being told what to do by elderly subalterns. I was sent about my business pretty smartly. I was to make out a report on the buildings and general lay-out of the camp and send them off at once, together with the woman Steinberg.

'Well, I did just that. Later, when the car was found wrecked and she disappeared, I was held to blame. Incompetence, they said, sending her off with just the driver as an escort. As if I could help it that the fool ran into a ditch.

'Anyway, I was posted home pretty quickly. Almost a court martial, they said. Later I suppose some nice efficient regular went over the camp with a toothcomb and found nothing.'

He stopped for a moment and brushed his forehead with a handkerchief.

'Yes, they found nothing. I don't know what, but they were on to something at that camp, before it was captured. If I'd had time I might have found it. But then I was bundled home, wasn't I? The only time in the whole war when I could have been of service to the country I was not allowed to.

'When I got back, I thought of taking the matter up at higher level, but what would have been the good? It was too late then, and in any case, I had a lot of personal troubles. My sister had died and Mary came to live with me.

'Oh! I see you're surprised, Mrs. Heath. No, she's not my daughter. It's just a little game we play together. It gives her pleasure and everybody has been so kind keeping up the pretence. So very kind.

'Well, my boy, so you want to know more about Steinberg. I'd love to know why, but then, I don't ask questions, do I? I only answer them. Very well, go ahead. Tell me what you want explaining and I'll see if I can help.'

'Thank you, sir.' Tony looked at the papers again.

'Now, you state here that in the compost beds were found traces of mycelium growths and other fungoid cultures. What others, Professor?'

'Oh, dear, so you don't even know that. I'm not certain, of course, I couldn't make a proper examination on the spot; but taken with the rest of the lay-out I should have thought it was obvious what they were.

'I stated, didn't I, that it appeared they were working on some form of fungoid mutation. Well, surely I don't have to tell you that the mushroom beds were merely incidental. The mushrooms themselves could only have been used for grafting. For giving body to some smaller and more active agent.

'Let's see just how good a biologist you are, Heath. Suppose you are planning to mutate a fungus to attack man. What would you use as your basic form? Surely a species that already had some leanings in that direction, wouldn't you? Something that would be willing to co-operate a little with you. Perhaps—'

He waited for Tony to speak.

'I see, I see, Professor,' his voice was eager and he was like a student. 'You mean Streptothra Madura.'

'Good boy, yes I think so, though it was impossible to be sure with the time and equipment I had, but it was either Madura or its next-of-kin Acinomycosis.

'A nice little creature Madura, Mrs. Heath. A neat, inoffensive fungus. Yet the disease it gives its name to, Madura Foot, is probably as unpleasant as anything we know in the tropics. A bare-footed native treads on this inoffensive little plant, and if the skin is at all thin or has a cut in it, the spores are pushed up into the flesh. I believe that once they have established themselves there, the only cure from a very nasty death is amputation.

'Yes, I think one could do something with Madura, you

know, Heath. It would be difficult, of course, but given a lot of time, a lot of equipment, and a lot of knowledge, I think one could. You would put your specimens under ultra violet rays, perhaps, possibly something else, I don't know. After a time, you might blend it with some larger form. The homely mushroom, for instance. And at last after a long line of generations you would produce something very odd. Something very potent and so horrible that the most unpleasant symptoms of Madura foot would look as trivial as a sprained ankle.'

'Yes, yes, it could be, it fits in,' said Tony. 'But tell me. Did you find anything to support the idea of ultra violet?'

'Oh dear me, no. As I said, all the equipment they could remove was gone. That was just my own theory, possibly quite wrong, too. There was nothing else left out. Even the bones were so charred as to be unrecognizable. Now I'm afraid there is nothing else I can tell you.'

'But, Professor,' Marcia broke in. 'Steinberg herself, what was she like, what did she say to you?'

'What was she like? It's difficult to say, my dear. She was so completely devoid of any definite personality. She was a smallish, rather mousey woman, about thirty I should say. She didn't seem to have any expression at all. I suppose there was something rather appealing about her in a way.

'They had taken away her clothes, and she was in battledress far too large for her. She had been shut up in one of the rooms in the living quarters of the camp when I saw her, and she didn't seem at all nervous, just completely indifferent. I couldn't make her out, I'm afraid. She wouldn't answer any of my questions, just stared woodenly at me and sometimes smiled.'

'But didn't she speak at all, surely she said something?'

'Oh yes, she spoke, but just at the end. After about half an hour of questioning her I went and rang through to H.Q. on the field telephone. What their reply was you know. I was to have Steinberg sent over to them that evening and wait for instructions.

'Well, I went back and told her that she was being moved at once. She was sitting on the steel bed in exactly the same position as I had left her. She seemed to take the news as a matter of course. She got up to go and then she looked at me and said—'

He paused suddenly.

'Yes, Professor,' she said, 'what did she say?'

He turned away from Tony and ran his tongue over his lips.

'I'm sorry. You see it's a little embarrassing for me. After all these years it's still embarrassing. She spoke in German. She said that she was glad to be going. That she had repeatedly asked to be taken to someone in authority, but she hoped my superiors were not as ignorant as I. If they were, they would probably waste a lot of time because they would never be able to understand the—it's hard to translate, *"Die Bestie die ich geschaffen habe"* '.

'What!' Tony looked wildly at him. 'She said that. She used that phrase.' He turned to Marcia. 'It fits, darling, it fits exactly. *"Die bestie, die Bestie die ich geschaffen habe."* Don't you see. The beast, darling, the Beast I have made.'

Very faint in the distance the cathedral clock struck seven. He got up.

'Thank you, Professor, you've been most helpful. Please let me know if you remember anything else.'

It was possible that Roberts knew more, but he had to let them have this at Farhill at once. That phrase confirmed their theory and he must get through to Hearn without delay. The point about Madura was vital. If it was correct and Hearn had a little time, they might still beat it at Farhill. But that was nonsense, they had no time.

'Very well, Professor, we'll go now.' He got to his feet and suddenly realized how weary he was. He looked at the bowed figure of Roberts, and prayed that he might remember something more. That the eyes would suddenly light up, the lips move and another vital point would be revealed.

But nothing came. The Professor opened the door and led them out into the hall.

There was a movement on the stairs and looking up they saw the thin figure of Mary staring down at them.

Although her body was hidden in the gloom, her head and shoulders stood out in the ray of light through the dusty casement window on the landing.

The face itself was heavy and dull. It was void of expression like an animal's, but somehow the eyes were alive behind her glasses. The eyes and the hair. Dark, rather beautiful eyes peered at them, and above the eyes, above the low, narrow forehead her hair was like red gold in the sunlight.

Roberts looked at her and his expression told them that it was not only for her sake that the father-daughter role was played.

'It's all right, my dear,' he said very gently, 'it's all right, it's only Mr. and Mrs. Heath and they're just going, don't worry. I'll be up in a moment.'

'Poor thing,' he said to Marcia, 'she's so nervous, you know. When she came here first she would hardly go outside her room. Now with these terrible murders and the children here— It's been difficult for her, very difficult.'

He pushed back the heavy door and held out his hand to Tony. 'Well, my boy, as I said, I'll let you know if I remember any more, I assure you of that. Now may I ask you one final question? Are we shortly to expect an outbreak of Madura Foot in this country?'

'I don't know, Professor,' said Tony slowly. 'I honestly don't know, but it could be, yes, it could be.'

He let go the hand and walked quickly down the path with Marcia beside him, to where the big car gleamed in the light.

The sun was up in the sky now and the blots and scars of the Old Town were once more revealed.

From tenements and basements a cloth-capped army was emerging cautiously into the daylight. A tram screamed up the hill before them as they wound through the shopping centre, and then as if suddenly walking from one room to another they were beneath the cathedral and driving across the quad.

They stopped in front of their house and for a moment neither of them made a motion of getting out.

Marcia laid her hand on Tony's arm and looked at him. 'Well, darling, has it helped at all?' They were the first words she had spoken since leaving Roberts's house.

'Yes, oh yes, quite a lot really, though it's probably too late. God, if the brass hats had listened to him in the beginning, they could have crushed this thing like an egg. But now, assuming it was Madura they used, it's going to be very difficult.

'If we had any idea of the degree of radiations they employed to start the mutations, it would be merely mathematics to work out a series which would turn back the process and render it innocuous. But we don't know, do we, and it's going to take a long, long time to find it.

'God! If the stupid, bloody fools had only listened to him in the first place, we could have smashed this thing in a week. You know, I was almost on the point of asking him to come and work with us. Telling him what was going on. It was only Kirk's orders that stopped me.'

'I know, darling. I felt that too. But in a way, don't ask me why, I'm glad you didn't. Anyway, let's go in. You've got to ring Hearn.'

The sun was streaming through the windows and the house looked bright and cheerful.

As the door swung shut behind them, they looked at each other and somehow managed to smile. Then, without speaking, Tony crossed to the phone and asked for the Farhill number.

Marcia waited for a moment and then left him. She knew exactly what would happen. He always gave his news to Hearn, they would discuss it, and then they would be off again. He would try to persuade her to stay in Durford, to go alone, but whatever happened she was going with him. In a very short time they would leave. But before that at least nobody could deny them a few minutes.

She ran up the stairs, hoping that her rebellion against economy had stood her in good stead. She was right. She put her hand inside the cistern cupboard and the heater was still on. She walked into the bathroom and turned the tap. The brown peaty water of Durford gushed out, hot and tingling.

She undressed carelessly, throwing her clothes to the floor, caring nothing for order or creases, and stepped down between the green walls of the bath. The water flowed round her like a cure. She felt all the drab soddenness of her tired body flowing away from her with the water, and was once more confident and alive.

For a long time she lay in the bath, and then got out slowly and stood on the mat, looking at herself in the glass, while the water ran down her firm breasts, and belly and flanks. She reached for a towel and turned and saw Tony looking at her.

'Well, darling, what did Hearn say, was he pleased?'

He didn't answer, but walked slowly towards her.

'Tony, don't be silly, we haven't any time, besides I'm soaking, you'll ruin your suit. Oh, Tony—'

She looked into his eyes and they were shining. With their light everything dropped away from her. The fear dropped, the horror dropped, 'the Beast I have made' dropped away and was nothing.

She opened her arms and her glistening body to him and for a moment there were no two happier people in the world than Tony and Marcia Heath.

CHAPTER TEN

VON ZULER dragged his steel foot across the lounge of the Four Seasons Hotel, and he looked what he was; very cold, very hard, and very efficient. He smelt slightly of scent, and the hand that took Trubenoff's was bright with rings.

He threw himself down on the sofa beside the Russian and smiled at him. There was a lot of gold in his smile.

'Well, my friend, I'm afraid I must apologize to you. I would so much have liked to meet you at the airport, but my masters are difficult people. It took a lot of time to persuade them to give me the powers we need. Ah, thank you.' He took the proffered glass and drained it in one swift movement.

'Anyhow, we are getting on. All the wheels are in motion, the spring is wound up, the hounds are ready. Somewhere the fox will be preparing to come out of its hole, and if it does, I shall hold it in the hollow of my hand.'

He spread his palm on the table and it was as dry and smooth as a lizard.

'Now I have done all I can, Herr Trubenoff, everything. Will you, in your turn, help me a little? Can you tell me why your General Kirk wants these people?'

'I'm sorry, Von Zuler, truly sorry. If it were up to Kirk personally I would tell you. He said that himself. Unfortunately, like you, he is merely a servant of his government. His orders were quite definite. At the moment nobody is to be told.'

'Very well, we will accept it. You are under orders from a higher authority, and we Germans respect authority. Perhaps it is our national vice, I don't know. Once someone called us a race of carnivorous sheep. He may have been right, I don't know.

'Anyway, I respect authority, therefore I respect your silence. Besides, I have an affection for your General. During the war we were almost opposite numbers, I suppose. He shot a great number of my people, and I—shall we say, I disposed of a great many of his. Still, that was long ago. The war is over, or is it? Is the war really over, Herr Trubenoff?'

Trubenoff looked very hard at him. 'Yes, the war is over. What I want you to do has no political or military significance whatsoever. That I promise you.'

'Good, with that assurance I can satisfy my masters. Every man, every car, every ear in my department is *à votre service*, my friend.

'But still it is going to be difficult, very difficult. I wonder, living as you have done in nice peaceful, democratic England, if you can realize just how difficult it may be.

'You want to find Rosa Steinberg. In forty-five your masters let her escape. Too many of our big fish were falling into their nets for them to bother much about her, and she was forgotten. Now you want her again. You also want the three men who were arrested with her at Ruhleben, Messrs. Wolf, Becker, and Tausch, and later released after short prison sentences. You want to interview these people and interview them quickly.

'Well, I'm afraid it may be impossible. I have been through all our records and so far as I know it is impossible. Tausch hanged himself on his release from prison and Wolf died of Bergers disease in '48. That leaves only one, Herr Trubenoff.'

Trubenoff lifted the decanter and refilled the glasses.

'I see, two dead, Wolf and Tausch, but there is still the third; what happened to Becker, Herr von Zuler?'

'Thank you.' Once more there was a quick, smooth movement and the glass was empty. He leaned back on the cushions and his words came very slowly.

'My friend, do you realize what Becker was? He was no scientist. He had only been at Ruhleben one month before it was taken. He was a concentration camp guard.

'Herr Trubenoff, do you know what that means? For years, since he was a boy, that man had been encouraged, paid, decorated by the state for one purpose. The infliction of suffering. He has gone from camp to camp over the years, and has indulged in abominations which are normally found only in criminal lunatic asylums. He has been rewarded for these crimes. Life for him has had only one problem, the problem of pain. That is his trade, his life, his métier, the only thing he understands.

'Now what happens to such a man? His world disintegrates. He is arrested and sent for trial. Very probably he wants to die, but because there is not much definite evidence against him, and your English masters worship evidence, he receives only a light sentence.

'He comes out free into the world after his sentence. Free to go and do what he likes except for one thing. The one thing he really knows, that he has been supported, applauded for doing is closed to him. He is a monster in a world he doesn't understand. He would change, don't you think? He would have to. His name is common, but given the right set of circumstances there could be a stigma about such a name. Even here in Germany there would be a stigma. He would change his name, but not only his name, his whole personality would have to change. He would become like a wiped slate.

'Our country is full of such people. A scientist can now be a bus driver, a catholic, a communist, a blond, dark. You must try and imagine how complete such a change might be. That is why it will be difficult, Herr Trubenoff. Don't worry, I shall find him, I shall find Kurt Becker, I promise you that; but will I find him in time?'

The waiter came noiselessly across the thick carpet and bowed deeply. He placed a slip of paper on to the table, bowed again, and was gone.

Von Zuler took up the paper and looked at it almost indifferently. Then he held it over his heavy gun metal lighter. He crumpled the ash very carefully and smiled his gold smile at Trubenoff.

'Well, mein Herr, we are getting on. You see before you a wonderful man, a miracle worker. I had a hunch, just a slight hunch, but it may be coming up. That little bit of ash makes me think it may be coming up.' He stirred the grey dust in the bowl.

'Don't be excited, though. I may still be wrong, but we have to follow it up. In any case I think I can promise you an interesting evening. Shall we go?'

He pulled himself to his feet and, his stiff leg trailing beside him, moved slowly to the door.

The driver looked about fourteen and was completely dressed in balloon fabric. He held open the door with a flourish and grinned slightly as Von Zuler barked an address at him.

The cab fled along the banks of the two Alster lakes, while the dying sun played on the façades of central Hamburg. They drove past block after block of new buildings and crossed bridges. Then they turned suddenly to the right towards the Elbe and the magnificent view of the enormous dockyards.

Trubenoff cared for no views. He sat rigidly beside Von Zuler and prayed that his hunch might succeed. He was completely out of his element. For years he had worked in Kirk's department and this was the first time he had gone out on a case. He had always regarded himself as a kind of human marshalling yard. People sent him scraps of information. Some trivial, some important. His job was to sort them out into their proper channels, weigh their value, and hand them over to Kirk.

That was what he was used to, what he fully understood, what he loved. Now he was sitting in the back of a car with a man he particularly disliked, on what might well be a mere wild goose chase. He didn't even know why Kirk wanted the information. He had merely been sent off to Germany at a moment's notice with orders to find a woman called Steinberg, whom he had never heard of, and given a list of questions which he was to put to any of her surviving assistants. All he knew was that the matter was too urgent and too secret to be dealt with by any normal method or agent. He cursed softly to himself as the car rattled over the cobbles.

They were among the ruins now. On either side torn, roofless houses stood against the sky. Blank walls loomed like follies; some of them fantastic, with baths and lavatory pans still hanging from their crumbling sides. Everywhere there

were the long stretches of bare, rubble-strewn ground waiting
for the new blocks of concrete flats to go up.

In front of them the sky was growing lighter. There was
a glow in the distance and the ruins began to stand out like
properties of a stage set, exaggerated by the arc lamps.

They turned a corner and a street stretched away from them.
A long, low street, alive with light like a phosphorous ribbon
in the dusk. From every side of it signs moved and neon tubes
flashed. It was like a fairground. It shuddered and heaved with
noise and movement. Traffic, motor horns, music, the shouts
of barkers outside the clubs.

Their driver added to the noise. He kept his hand hard down
on his horn and with tyres screaming pulled across the road
and drew up at the pavement of the Reperbahn, the Rope Walk,
the greatest street of entertainment in the world.

The commissionaire was gigantic in his uniform and he
handed the two men out of the car as if they were expensive
and fragile pieces of merchandise. Trubenoff shook his protect-
ing hand away almost fiercely, and followed Von Zuler across
the pavement towards the blazing entrance of the club.

*

Unter der Kaserne, vor dem grossen Tor,
  Stebt eine Lanterne—
. Through the smoke, the huge, red room shuddered and
heaved with the march, the crash of the beer mugs beating in
time on the tables and the feet of the dancers crushed together
on the tiny glass stage.

He paused in the entrance as the girl took his coat and looked
into the hall. It was like a descent into hell. On all sides of the
room of plush and gold, the garish lights lit up the cheap
decorations, the streamers, and the terrible faces.

Balloons waved in front of him on the rising smoke and
suffocating air, obscuring his view, but he knew them; they
were the same faces. Young and old, blond or dark, bloated or
lean, it was the same face watching him through the smoke.
The face of the war.

The same immeasurably old, sad, resigned, yet hysterical face
peered at him from every side and its habits hadn't changed
at all.

The boys still sat with the boys and the girls with the girls.
The couples on the stage were not enjoying themselves, they
were not dancing. They were desperately in earnest. They were
soldiers and they were marching to war. Each head was bent
low as though in prayer, as the stiff military rhythm rose and

fell. They were marching in the pursuit of gaiety, the last drop of excitement, the height of a good time.

'These people can never do anything in moderation,' he thought, as he walked through the gin fumes, sweat, and cigar smoke. 'Whatever they do it must always be a little too thorough, a little too near the last futile extreme.'

He shouldered his way after Von Zuler towards the table that a bowing head waiter was motioning them to.

'Ah, this is excellent, my dear colleague. Quite a good table.' Von Zuler gave his order and then smiled at the Russian.

'You know, my friend, I feel that you are somehow ill at ease. You hate this, don't you? What you like is a nice. cosy office in safe London. A drink, perhaps, in a quiet club with a few chosen friends. But now you have to sit in a place like this with a dreadful, talkative fellow who uses scent. Is that not what you were thinking, my friend?'

In spite of himself Trubenoff had to smile, the German had too closely echoed his thoughts.

'But still, we have not come here merely to enjoy ourselves, I am afraid. As I said, I have a hunch and this is where we might start to test it. I have brought you here to show you what we are up against.'

He waved his hand in front of him taking in the whole room. ' "What have we come into the wilderness to see," the Jewish Bible says, I believe. Well, look into this wilderness, mein Herr, and think what you have asked me to do.

'I didn't bring you here for fun. We are both too old to sit watching half-naked girls. No, I wanted you to see the possible hiding place of somebody like Kurt Becker.

'Look around you. Look at every face in this room, and most of them over thirty will have something to hide. All over Germany in clubs like this you will find them, the secret people, and I have to pick one of them, out of the haystack, as you say.'

Trubenoff did not reply, but looked around the room at the faces in the room. He tried to picture them as they must have been years ago, in uniforms of black and grey. A little younger, a little firmer, a little more arrogant, but still essentially the same. And was there one of them, he wondered, one amongst all the faces in the room who had once stood guard over a mushroom bed, at the bidding of a girl scientist?

The music had changed now. The marching feet had stopped, and the band was playing a long ago American dance tune. The saxophonist stood on the front of the stage and the spotlight gleamed on his instrument and his dark, oily hair. His face was a boy's face under the make-up. It was as white as something that had been shut away for years.

'Don't know why, there's no sun up in the sky, stormy weather.' Trubenoff, who hated music and jazz in particular, had to listen. The notes were harsh and discordant, but there was something terribly sad and haunting about the playing of that screaming tune.

.'Since my love and I aren't together.'

It was like a pain in his head. His love was dead years ago and he had expelled her picture from his mind, but this music, played by a degenerate in a sordid club of the nation that had killed her, was bringing it back.

The rhythm rose suddenly to its final crescendo and then sank slowly away.

'Keeps raining all the time.'

The final note died and the musician bowed to the deafening applause like a wan black flower.

'Well, *prosit*, my friend,' said Von Zuler thickly. 'At least let us enjoy ourselves while we can, even though we are working. I don't think you like music very much, you know, but perhaps that tune took you back a little. Back before, what is it? "Those old, unhappy, far-off days and battles long ago." He can play, too, that boy, I suspect he is the only real asset that this rat-hole of a club has left.

'Ah, waiter, there you are. My friend is from England, and is very anxious to meet the saxophone player. Perhaps you would be kind enough to give him this.'

He took a visiting card from his pocket, scrawled a few words on it, and then handed it to the man.

Trubenoff wanted to protest. He had no desire to talk to any musician, no desire to sit in this club and drink the harsh schnapps before him, but something in his companion's manner stopped him. Von Zuler was suddenly stripped of all his urbanity as of a glove, and his hard eyes were fixed on the bandstand like a pointing gun dog's.

Trubenoff watched the waiter walking across the room. The saxophonist leaned against the backcloth talking to the pianist. All the fire seemed to have left him, and it was impossible to believe that it was he who had played that screaming tune.

He put out a limp hand and took the card indifferently. He glanced at it, and then turned it over and read the pencilled notes on the back.

Suddenly he stiffened. As if jerked by a wire the body tightened. He craned forwards and stared hard across the room at Von Zuler. Then he turned on his heels and moved like a deer to the door at the back of the platform.

'Ah!' Von Zuler pushed aside his glass and stood up. 'Well, I am very sorry, but I'm afraid that that is the end of the party. It seems that my little hunch is about to come off after all. A pity, because a few more drinks would have been pleasant. But still I think I can show you something worth while. Shall we go?'

The police car swept through the bright night with its siren blaring. It slowed at no corners, it stopped at no intersections or traffic lights, it gave way to no one. A tiny, metallic voice from a radio gave the driver his instructions, and a few minutes later they pulled up before a grim block of working class flats. A plain clothes man stood by the kerb and opened the door. 'Number Twelve, Herr Commandant. I don't think he knew he was being followed. He ran straight into the taxi and didn't look round at all. Schmidt is waiting on the landing, second floor.'

The door of Number Twelve was chipped and marked with the scars of years. It was bolted on the inside.

Von Zuler gave an order to the burly detective who stood outside it, and stood to one side.

The man moved back and then ran at the door. His shoulder seemed to press for a moment against the rotten wood, almost as if he leaned against it. Then, with a sudden jerk, the lock fell away and the door was open.

The room itself came as a shock to Trubenoff. As they had come up the stairs he had noted the slum character of the building. The chipped walls with the obscenities scrawled upon them. The general air of decay and neglect. The room he now entered was light and brightly painted. The furniture was new and gleaming with polish. There were flowers on the white oak table and it was as fresh and as clean as a hospital ward.

It was like a hospital in another way too. Under the flower scent came the unmistakable odour, half antiseptic and half something else, the odour of the sick room.

He walked a little way into the room and then stopped at the voice. 'Stay where you are,' said the voice. 'Stay very still, just where you are now, and don't move at all.'

The musician leaned against the door at the back of the room. His left hand was tight on the door-handle and his right hand held a large blue automatic. It shook slightly in his thin, white hand.

'Don't be a silly boy, Karl.' Von Zuler's voice was very gentle. 'Don't be silly, nobody is going to hurt you. There's no point in being silly. No point at all.'

He completely ignored the gun and walked across the room, his false leg dragging behind him on the carpet.

'Get back, get back, I'll kill you if you go near the door.'
The boy's voice was a scream now.

'You're not going to kill anybody, Karl. You can't kill anybody. You haven't the strength to kill anybody. Go on and
try. You can't even pull the trigger, can you, Karl?'

Trubenoff watched him. He watched him slowly dragging
himself across the carpet towards the boy, talking as he went.
He was almost up to him. He was at arm's length from him
when the thin finger started to whiten on the trigger. In a
tenth of a second the gun had to go off. It was as near as that,
when Von Zuler struck. He seemed to brace himself, draw
himself together, and then his false leg shot forward like a
piston straight into the musician's groin, while his ringed hand
slashed across the falling face.

The detective kicked the gun to the side and then lifted the
boy from the floor and held him in front of Von Zuler. The
police chief put out his hand and slowly stroked the bleeding
face.

'This is Karl, Herr Trubenoff,' he said. 'Karl is a nice boy,
he plays very well. We have nothing at all against Karl. He has
only one small fault, he makes friends too easily. That's a good
fault in itself. It's nice to have friends, but you should be
careful who your friends are, shouldn't you, Karl?' His hand
shot out again and again like a whip, and when he stopped
there were other marks on the white face.

'You have a sick friend, haven't you, Karl? Very sick, dying
of consumption in fact. He should be in a sanatorium, but
you don't want that, do you? You think you would die yourself if your friend left you. So what do you do, Karl? You
hide him away, don't you? You hide him and nurse him yourself. Every second you can spare you look after him. Always
dreading the day when the medical authorities will take him
away. That's why when a stranger in a club sends you a note
saying that the ambulance is already at the door, you leave
everything and take us straight to him.

'And now, Herr Trubenoff, will you please go through that
door. As I said, I respect your confidence and I will wait outside. I may be wrong in my hunch even now, but I don't
think so. There was once a man who had consumption. He
also had a boy friend who played a saxophone. He also had a
proper name. A man with that name was a guard at Ruhleben
once, under Miss Steinberg. He is all yours.' He pushed the
door open and waved Trubenoff through.

*

92

Although the room was in semi-darkness, it was quite clear that the man was dying. The face on the pillow was almost without flesh and the eyes were globes in their bone sockets. There were dark stains on the sheets too.

Trubenoff pulled a chair beside the bed and bent over him. His German was very correct and very soft.

'You are Kurt Becker,' he said, 'and you were once a guard at Ruhleben camp. Is that not so?'

The feverish eyes looked up at him, but they gave no sign of understanding.

'Listen to me, Becker. I am a British officer and there are two things that you must tell me.

'First, how far had Steinberg got with her experiments when the camp was captured? I know you told the authorities at the time that you had no knowledge of what was going on, but now you are dying and you have to tell me.

'Secondly, what happened to Steinberg and the records of her work?'

The dying eyes still gave no flicker of intelligence.

Trubenoff hardened his heart and went to the door.

He motioned to the plain clothes man and the boy was held struggling in the doorway, the light shining on his bleeding face. He turned once more to the bed.

'That is your friend, Becker. He has looked after you, nursed you, supported you, loved you. Now you must help him. He is in great trouble. He has threatened a police officer. They will take him to prison. But if you tell me what I want to know I will see he gets off lightly. That I promise you.'

Still there was no reply, no sign.

He motioned them away, shut the door, and played his last card. 'Becker, S.S. man Becker, number nine seven five one Becker. Tell me what happend to Steinberg. How did she escape, where did she go?' His German was as harsh and loud as a Prussian drill sergeant. 'I order you in the name of the Reich and the Führer to answer me, Becker. What happened to Steinberg?'

The eyes turned sharply to him. They lit up. The body seemed to stretch up towards him, and slowly and painfully the grey lips began to speak.

CHAPTER ELEVEN

'I SEE, then that is quite definite. You're sure. Thank you, Igor, you've done very well, very well indeed. What you've told me is of the greatest possible help. We have something to go on now. Yes, of course, give my thanks to Von Zuler and come back as soon as you like. Goodbye.'

Kirk dropped the phone back into its cradle, and smiled at his companions.

'Well, my friends, as they say across the channel, *ça marche*, we are getting on. That was my man in Germany. He has managed to run one of Steinberg's assistants to ground, and that assistant has talked. I will tell you what he said in a moment, but first what about Roberts, did you learn anything fresh from him? Are you any nearer?'

There was a complete change of atmosphere in the office. The feeling of slight suspicion and hostility between Hearn and Kirk had disappeared, as had the sense of helplessness. They sat round the table, irk, Hearn, Tony, and Marcia, and they were four comrades fighting, and possibly winning together. All awkwardness and formality had gone.

'Yes, General,' said Hearn. 'At last we seem to be making some progress. Tony's talk with Roberts was most useful ; vital in fact.

'It was Madura, of course, we are quite sure of that now, though changed by radiation ; changed out of all recognition. But we have something to go on. It had been subjected over a number of generations to ultra violet, to make it take its present form. There is no possible doubt about that. All we have to do is to find the exact degree of radiations used, and cancel them. Once we have done that, we can give the details to the authorities and our work is finished.'

'Just a moment, Doctor, you mean exactly that?' Kirk leaned forward excitedly. 'You mean that once you have the information about the radiations you can stop it?'

'Well, not quite. What I mean was that given the degree of radiation, the exact degree, we can develop a means of checking the further spread. It will take time, of course, and a lot of life will be lost, but in the end we will win. I'm quite certain of that.'

'I see, then it amounts to this. If you know the radiations used, we have at least a fighting chance. If not, you are helpless. Now tell me, how long do you consider it will take you to find what we want?'

'I don't know, I honestly don't know. It might be weeks, it might be months. I can't commit myself.'

'Fair enough. Now as I see it, the position is quite simple. Given the time, you could find your remedy in the laboratory, and be ready to deal with this thing, when and if it reaches this country. But you haven't got enough time, have you? You need weeks. You haven't got them. All you've got is four days. The meteorological office have just been through to me. Your spores are carried by the wind, aren't they? Well, in four days' time the wind is going to blow from the East.'

'Then you mean it's no good, we're finished anyway.' Hearn sank back in his chair.

'Oh no, we're not finished. We're going to beat it, because you're going to have the information you need before the wind changes.'

He got up from his chair and looked out of the window at the fields and the gardens and the waving trees.

'Yes, you're going to get it all right. Right from the horse's mouth, right from the founder of the feast. Right from Steinberg herself.

'This is what I heard from my man in Germany.

'As you know, we captured three of her associates at Ruhleben. Two of them, Wolf and Tausch, died; but one, Becker lived. He lived just long enough to give my friend a very valuable piece of information. He told my friend that there was a fourth man at Ruhleben who was intimate with Steinberg. A man who got away.

'This man, his name was then Loser, saw Becker after he came out of prison and had a long talk with him. He told Becker he was certain that Steinberg was alive, and he knew where she had gone. He also said that he was soon going to leave Germany himself and told him where he was going.

'Well, yesterday I saw Herr Paul Loser, the man who got away, and if I play my cards right, I think he will lead Miss Steinberg right into my net.'

*

Before he had even heard from Trubenoff, Kirk was already sure that Marcia was right. Steinberg was the quarry and Steinberg was alive.

Once the first phone call had come from Hamburg he was

certain. Somewhere she existed. Somewhere in Germany, Europe, America. Even in Russia itself, working as a slave labourer perhaps, carrying her knowledge with her, biding her time till a chance presented itself and then one fine morning—

Well, she existed and he was on his way to her now. The dying words of one of her assistants had given him a lead to another. Trubenoff had only been a few minutes in Von Zuler's office and they had soon told him that five years ago a certain Paul Loser had indeed left Germany. He had left with a visa for England.

Back in London the pieces had come together with a rush. Two phone calls, a few scraps of paper, a whispered word in the right quarter, and he was off.

There was no fuss about it. No hurry. He took no assistants. He was just an elderly gentleman in a tight coat and an over-heated car, driving out into the green heart of England, as if for pleasure.

He drove slowly cursing the traffic on the Great West Road and then turned off into the wandering byways north of Maidenhead, leaning back in his seat and enjoying the scenery.

After a time he stopped his car before a pub in a low white village, and went into the bar.

He chatted pleasantly to the landlord and bought a round of drinks.

'Decent old boy,' thought the locals, and they talked freely before him, answering his innocent questions without embarrassment. After a time he got up from the bar stool, thanked the landlord, nodded an affable farewell to all and sundry, and once more went out to his car.

For about a mile he followed the road and then turned sharply up a lane which ran beside a stream. It wound steeply up the hillside, the water burbling beside it, and its ditches were bright with flowers. At the top of the hill it ended abruptly in two white gates dazzling in the sunshine.

The hedges beside the gates were trim and obviously cut by a professional, while the lawn behind them was as smooth as a mower advertisement. At the end of the lawn stood a long, wonderfully graceful Georgian house.

He drove the car smoothly across the chipped drive to the front door, got out, and pushed the gleaming bell push.

The maid who opened the door was a relic of a forgotten age. The frilled white cap, the starched cuffs, the tight cellulose belt would all have warmed Mrs. Beeton's hearts, as would the look of inquiring deference.

She took his card, glanced at it, looked him up and down and as if deciding that he was a respectable person, led him across an antler-hung hall into a drawing-room.

The room was beautiful. It was filled with flowers and gleamed with brass and polished furniture. He stood exactly in the centre of the big carpet. He held his hat in his hands and kept his overcoat on, as he looked at the lustre around him. The lustre which he had come to tarnish.

He looked enormous and threatening as he stood there, his face heavy and set, his hands clenched at his side. A bull in the china shop.

'General Kirk, what can I do for you? I am Mrs. Haversfield.' He turned very slowly and looked at the woman who had come silently into the room. She was worth looking at.

She was very slight and thin, almost gaunt it might be said, and she was long past her youth, but there were still traces of a great beauty about her. Her hair was turning grey and was swept high back above her ears. Her violet eyes were wide and untroubled. She looked completely at her ease. Yet there was something about her eyes and her expression. Something that age had not put there and which no careful make-up could ever alter.

'You asked to see my husband, I believe. I'm afraid he is not a very fit man these days. He sees very few people. Perhaps I can help you.' The voice was low and soft and yet commanding.

'Perhaps you can, Madam, perhaps you can. I'm sure in many ways you could help me. But just at the moment I do not require your assistance. I did not ask for it. As I told your maid, I merely wish to see your husband.'

Kirk was usually the most courteous of men, but he spoke like a boor.

The woman froze for a moment as if he had struck her across the face. Then she crossed the room and reached for the bell pull.

'I wouldn't do it if I were you, Madam. You can, of course. You are quite at liberty to call for your servants and have me thrown out, but I wouldn't, Mrs. Haversfield, or should I say Mrs. Paul Loser?'

Her fingers opened around the silken cord and her hand fell back to her side.

'Very well, what is it you want? At least tell me that before you see him. You are from the immigration people, I suppose.'

'No, not the immigration people. Not this time. This is my department.' He handed her his identity card.

She glanced at it and then gave it back to him.

'But I don't understand. Foreign Office Intelligence. What can you want with Paul? Oh God! Why can't he be left alone? When he first came here I could understand these official visits, but now, after five years.

'Don't you understand, five years. This is his home. The people here like him. Can't he have a little peace? He has paid for anything he did years ago.'

'Do you think so, Madam? Do you really think so? I don't. I don't believe he could even begin to pay, if he lived a thousand years. Now, will you please take me to him.'

'Very well, General, come with me.' All the fight had gone out of her. 'Come with me, but I beg you please be gentle with him. Whatever you say, Paul was never a bad man. Anything he did, he was made to do. I knew him before the war, you know. We lost track of course, but later when he wrote to me that he was ill I went out to Germany at once. We were married shortly afterwards.

'General Kirk, my family is very old and has given a lot of service to this country. My name is a good name. I give you my word that since we were maried Paul has never had one minute's peace thinking of the things they made him do. Now will you follow me.'

A girl in a nurse's uniform was sitting beside the sick man; she moved away as they approached.

The wheel chair had been put at the end of the terrace. From the chair the man looked out with sunken eyes across the Thames valley, towards the Chilterns.

Every day he sat like that. Completely motionless, completely without expression, gazing out towards those far, grey hills, as if he had already left his chair and his sick body for their slopes. He looked up, smiled gently at his wife, listened to her whispered explanation, and then motioned Kirk to a bench beside the chair.

The woman bowed to Kirk and all the lines in her face seemed to speak to him. Then she turned and walked back to the house. Her body was stiff and rigid and she was like a corpse walking in the sunlight.

The man in the chair fumbled in the folds of his rug. He drew out a packet of cigarettes. With shaking hands he offered it to Kirk.

The General took one and waited for Loser to speak first. When the words came, they were thick and guttural and the English was badly formed.

'Well, General, what do you want with me? My wife tells me you are from the Foreign Office. I presume it is about my naturalization application. I thought I had given all the particulars necessary.'

'No, Loser,' Kirk spoke in German and his voice was very hard. 'Not about your naturalization. Far from it, but it could be about your deportation.

'As you know, I represent Foreign Office Intelligence. My department has recently learned that we want you, Herr Loser. We want you in connexion with certain war crimes which you are thought to be concerned with at Ruhleben camp.'

'So, at last.' The man's voice showed no fear, only great tiredness. 'Yes, I was at Ruhleben, General. I concealed that. I got away before the camp was taken by your troops. I was with Steinberg. But one thing I promise you, I had nothing to do with the running of the camp, nothing to do with the human experiments. I was merely on the outside, merely concerned with security. That was all. Well, eleven years pass, and now it comes out. What will you do to me, General Kirk? There is not a great deal you can do really. I am dying of paralysis in any case.'

Kirk looked at him, looked past him at the far hills and his voice was gentle again.

'I won't do anything to you, Loser. I won't do anything at all. As you say, it's a long time ago. We don't want the expense of a trial, and besides we don't want to try a dying man. All we shall do is to determine where you die.'

'Where? I don't understand.'

'Don't you? Your naturalization papers are not yet complete, I think. You have no claim on us yet. You were born in Breslau, I believe. That makes you a citizen of the East German People's Republic, doesn't it? You will fly there within forty-eight hours, that I promise you. Born in Breslau, died in Breslau, eh, Herr Loser!'

'But you can't, no, you can't do it. No, you must try me here. You musn't send me back. You musn't. You don't know those people. You don't know what they'll do to me. You can't do it, Herr General.' His voice was a scream now.

'Believe me, I can, I shall, and I do know what they will do to you.' Kirk smiled gently at him.

'There is, however, one way in which this unpleasant contingency can still be avoided. One little thing which can make me leave you now and forget all about you, walk away from you now and forget all about you again.'

'But I don't understand. Tell me what way, what do you want? I'll do anything, anything at all.'

'Good, we're beginning to understand each other, I think. I

want you to answer two questions. Two easy questions, that is all. When you have answered them I shall leave and there will be no plane to Breslau. Are you ready?'

The sick man nodded eagerly.

'Good. Now tell me, Loser, you were in Steinberg's confidence I believe.'

'In her confidence. That is nonsense, General. Nobody could be in her confidence. If you'd known her you would see that I am speaking the truth. She had no contact with anything human. She was not a person it was possible to have contact with.'

'And yet you saw her after her escape, didn't you? You saw her and you told you how she had escaped, and where she was going, didn't she? You told Becker that, didn't you, Loser? No, don't deny it, just think of Breslau and answer my questions. They're very easy. Firstly, how did Steinberg escape, and secondly where did she propose to go after her escape? After you saw her.'

Loser shook his head very slowly and looked straight in front of him away from Kirk.

'No, General, I cannot answer your questions. I never saw her after her escape. Becker was lying. I told him nothing. But he told me how she got away. He told me that a stupid British soldier who couldn't drive ran his jeep into a ditch and killed himself. That was how the Fräulein escaped, Herr General. That is all I know.'

'It is you who are lying, Loser, not Backer. You did see her, and you do know where she went. I'll give you one more chance to answer my questions and then I shall leave you. One more chance and then Breslau, Loser.'

The German looked at him and he was once more completely self possessed.

'Very well then, so be it. Breslau it is. I shall probably die on the journey, and in any case I cannot tell you what I don't know. Goodbye for the present, Herr General Kirk.'

Without a word Kirk got up and left him. As he walked across the terrace he saw the little nurse cross towards the wheel chair where the man sat completely motionless, looking at the far hills.

Above him a plane droned slowly eastwards.

The woman was waiting for him in the hall, the half-drawn curtains shading her ravaged face. The great violet eyes seemed to look right through him.

'Well, General, have you found out what you wanted, can we at last have a little peace?'

'Peace, yes, Madam, you can have peace. All the peace you

100

want.' His voice sounded completely indifferent. 'I have talked to your husband. I have offered him peace here, although I know him to be a war criminal. I have asked him to do something for me in return. To answer two simple questions and then I promised to leave him alone.'

'And has he told you? Has he answered your questions?' Her words were purely rhetorical, she already knew the answer.

'No, he has not. Therefore I would advise you to pack his things. He has deliberately withheld information necessary to the safety of my country. Therefore I consider him to be an unfit person to remain here any longer. I shall see that he leaves Great Britain within forty-eight hours from now. You will get your peace then, Madam, as soon as I put him on the plane to Breslau.'

'To Breslau, you, you devil!' All the air of breeding fell away from her face like chalk on a blackboard. Her voice kept its beautiful tones, but the words were the coarse brutal words of the streets. She stood in the dim graceful hall among the flowers and the polished furniture and cursed and swore, and then suddenly spat in his face.

Kirk never moved or altered his expression. He just looked indifferently at her, not even bothering to wipe the spittle that hung on his cheek.

She stopped as suddenly as she had begun. Her words stopped as if she had been gagged and she bent over the chair back sobbing. After a time, she turned her tear-stained face to him.

'General Kirk,' she said. 'I am not going to ask you to forgive me for what I have said or done. No forgiveness is possible. I will, however, ask you one thing. Please try and understand that if you kill him by sending him to East Germany, you will kill me also, as definitely as if you put a bullet through my head.'

Kirk bowed and did not reply.

'You would not mind that now. I don't blame you, but at least tell me what was the question you want answered. He might tell me.'

'Ask him yourself, Mrs. Haversfield. Ask him yourself. I have no more time here. He knows the question, I am almost sure he knows the answer. If I get that answer by, shall we say, six o'clock the day after tomorrow, he will have nothing to fear from he. If not, it will be the plane, Mrs. Haversfield.'

'But you're not sure. You're not even sure he knows what you want and yet you will send him away just the same.'

'Yes, whether he knows or not, I will send him away, just

the same. All that can save him is the answer to my question, before those forty-eight hours are up. You have my office address on the card I gave you.

'Then goodbye, Mrs. Haversfield, until six o'clock the day after tomorrow.'

He walked past her out into the sunlight and got into his car. A little way down the lane he stopped and wiped his face. Then he threw the soiled handerchief far from him into a ditch, rank with henbane and nettles.

*

'And you think he'll talk.' Marcia leaned forward towards him, and her eyes were very bright.

'Yes, my dear, he'll talk. He doesn't want to and I imagine that he is so sick that he doesn't mind much where or when he dies. But he'll talk. That woman will make him talk. She minds. She'll see that he talks.'

'Always assuming that he knows, General,' Hearn broke in. 'You're not quite sure, are you?'

'No, I'm not sure, but very nearly. Becker said he knew and Becker wasn't lying. We're certain of that. When they met after Becker came out of jail, Loser told him that he knew how Steinberg had escaped and where she was planning to go. He made Becker swear on oath that he would never tell anyone about this. It was only by pretending to be a Nazi official that my man managed to get him to talk when he was delirious. Yes, I'm almost sure that Loser knew what happened to Steinberg.'

'And if you're right. If he does know and he does tell you what happened,' Tony spoke half to himself. 'How long will it take to get the figures we want? I mean it may be a long time. After all, as you yourself said, she may be anywhere. Russia, Europe, America, even here, anywhere in the world.'

Kirk placed his three fingers on the large globe that stood on the desk and slowly turned it.

'Yes, as you say, she may be anywhere. Anywhere in the world. But if Loser talks, and if he knows where she went, I shall have the information you want within twelve hours of his talking. That I promise you. That I stake my whole reputation upon.

'My friends, I am only the head of one department of one country. But in this, every intelligence service of every country of the world is at my disposal. I have only to lift the phone and ask one of my colleagues to help me, and if I can tell him why I want her and where she is, she will be picked up and will give you the information you want. Anywhere on this.' The globe swirled like a top under his hand.

'Then it amounts to this. It all hangs on Loser. If he talks and talks soon, we have a chance.'

'That, of course, I don't know. All I can do is to give you a piece of information that you ask me for. When I have given you that I've done and it will be up to you, gentlemen.'

'Fair enough, General. Let us have those figures about the radiations used and we'll break it, won't we, old man?' Tony smiled at Hearn, who nodded, started to speak and then paused as the phone rang beside him. 'Ah, excuse me a moment, please. Hullo, yes, that's right, this is the director speaking. Who is that? I see, yes, you were quite right, doctor. Just one minute.' He reached out for pencil and paper.

'Now, when did you say? Two hours ago. Will you please let me have the exact symptoms then. Yes, in detail.'

For a long time he listened to the voice at the end of the line, and his hand travelled across the paper.

"Thank you, Dr. Jacques, yes. I've got it. Now I want you to listen to me very carefully, please. The patient must be put into complete isolation at once. Complete isolation. Not even a doctor or a nurse with her. You understand that. Good. Also all persons who have been in contact with the case during the last forty-eight hours must be isolated . . .

'Good God, man, you'll have to find the power. This is vital. You're the Medical Officer in the area, aren't you? Yes, of course I'm sending someone down to you. Yes, right away. Very well, thank you for calling. Goodbye.'

He dropped the instrument back on to its rack and looked at Kirk.

'That was a small hospital on the North-East coast. When we first knew about this business we sent a circular out to all area medical officers, telling them to let us know if they encountered any out of the way or unknown diseases. The man on the end of that phone has almost exactly described the thing we have in there.'

He nodded towards the door and a muscle twitched in the corner of his mouth as he finished speaking.

'It seems that after all we won't have to wait for that wind, General.'

CHAPTER TWELVE

THERE is said to be a black sheep in every family, and though that may be true for a great deal of humanity, there are always exceptions. One exception was the Sopers.

Among the Soper descendants there was no name which could not be referred to. There were no staring black spaces in the family album to proclaim the downfall of Uncle William or Great Aunt Madge. All the Sopers were entirely as they should be, for they were not as other men.

In Mrs. Soper's trim, if somewhat cheerless, villa, grim in side whiskers, the fathers of nonconformity stared down at the occasional guest. The bookcase was full of works of instruction and spiritual betterment. The family album bulged with photographs of honest tradesmen and ministers of God, and towards the end with prim children clutching diplomas. The Sopers were a beacon of rectitude in the neighbourhood.

It was a beautiful morning, and as Harriet Soper cycled through the breaking sunshine, everything was lovely around her. The fields were a pale yellow and swaying in the breeze. The trees were greener than the greenest green, the hedgerows were bright with flowers, and in the distance she could just make out the blue carpet of the sea.

Harriet cared for none of these things. The countryside was all very well in its way, another example of the munificence of the Creator, but other matters were more important. Her mind was on her work.

Although she had plenty of time in hand, she rode her sedate bicycle as if her life depended on it.

She had only been two months at Shepherd's Store, and she meant to keep the good impression she had created. It was true that at the moment she was just a counter assistant, but with strict punctuality and marked attention to duty, she might one day become more. Why, only last week old Mr. Shepherd himself had remarked how pleased he was with her. A glorious vision of her future stretched ahead and she cherished his words with pride, for apart from being her employer, Mr. Shepherd was a great man.

He was an elder of the chapel, a County Councillor, a Justice of the Peace, the Liberal candidate at the last election, and a thorn in the side of all desecrators of the Sabbath.

Her thin, black cotton legs redoubled their efforts on the pedals, and a few minutes later she was speeding through the streets of the little market town to draw up at the store entrance.

It was not only routine duty that made Harriet so early. True it was Wednesday, half day. A lot of the staff came earlier than usual on Wednesdays, hoping to have their counters in such apple pie order that they could leave dead on time, but she had no interest in such unworthy motives. She had only the good of the firm at heart, the good of the firm and possibly just a little something else, a slight feeling of excitement, which made her eager to get to work. For Wednesday was the day, the day it happened, the day things happened.

It had been going on for a long time now. Every Wednesday there had been a small number of discrepancies. Nothing much. A kettle here, a pair of socks there, but there was always something. It was wrong, very wrong. Mr. Shepherd thought it was wrong. He was so concerned that he was thinking of employing a store detective. He had said so to the under manager, who had told Harriet.

Well, she didn't think they needed a detective. What they needed was her, Harriet, because she was almost sure she knew who it was.

Every Wednesday, just about ten o'clock, a large, stout woman, carrying a multitude of shopping baskets, was in the habit of coming into the store. She walked briskly round it, rummaging among every counter, and although she appeared to buy nothing, she always seemed to go out a little heavier, a little more burdened, than she had come in.

Harriet was certain it was the fat woman, and she meant to stop it. Today she would arrange her counter, moving goods to the side so she had an uninterrupted view of the whole building, and if she saw that woman take so much as a button, she would stop her. It was her clear duty to do so. However trivial the missing articles might be, the fat woman must be arrested and punished. She must be made to see how very wrong it was to take them, to realize that she had no right to those socks, crockery, and oddments, that they were not hers, but Mr. Shepherd's. For her own sake she must be made to see it.

Grim-faced as a crusader, Harriet placed her bicycle in the rack and strode into the store.

*

Wednesday morning was usually busy, and that day was no exception. Crowds of women had come in from the outlying villages and invaded the shops, so that the girls behind the counters were rushed off their feet. They fumed and fretted, and inwardly cursing the slower and more difficult customers, stared at the clock. Harriet did not curse. Cursing was an abomination in the sight of the Lord, and she was civil, if a little preoccupied. She did, however, look at the clock from time to time, though for very different reasons.

It was half past eleven, and nothing had happened, nothing at all. No large, bustling figure had appeared through the doors, striding purposefully down the rows, rummaging untidily among the counters and then moving on without a single purchase. It was all very annoying. She turned impatiently to attend to a customer and then suddenly stiffened.

She paused in the very act of handing change, and stared down the aisle. There was no stout woman in sight this time, but there was something. There was a stout child. A stout, bullet-headed boy of about ten was busily going through the hosiery stall, in a familiar and purposeful manner.

There was something terribly alike in his actions and those of her suspect ; there must be a connexion. There was. As she watched, she suddenly saw him make a deft movement with his hand, and a pair of thick, woollen socks seemed to glide by their own will beneath his bulging jacket.

Harriet acted quickly. She ignored the need for letting a thief leave the premises, and brushing past her astonished customer, ran down the aisle, her feet slipping madly on the polished floor, and seized him by his short bristly hair as he moved to the shoe department.

It was as if a spring had been released. The bullet head jerked round on its shoulders and she was confronted with a round freckled face, bearing an expression of such malignity that for a second she released her grip.

With a tug, the bristle hair was pulled from her grasp and the thick figure broke away and careered like a miniature tank down the aisle.

For such a stout person, he moved with surprising speed. He rounded a corner, hurling two customers heavily and painfully to the ground. His shoulder caught the corner of a rack piled high with crockery that sank with a noise of breaking ruin. A muscular shop walker vaulted over the counter towards him, slipped on the lino, and collided with a stand of tinned peas. Everywhere there was chaos and still the small figure fled on. He was almost at the entrance now. In front of him the three brass-rimmed steps lead up to the sunlight and freedom. He must make it. The doors were open, his nearest pursuer was far behind him, there was nothing to stop him. He had to make it.

And then suddenly the door was no longer open. It was as if the doorway had been suddenly blanked out by cloth. There was no entrance now, no way of escape. No hope.

He looked over his shoulder. The pursuers were gaining; he paused for a split second, turned to the right and then doubled back. He was too late, there was only one way, one hope, he had to take it. He bent his body like a ball, lowered his head and charged. He charged at the dark shape, aiming exactly at the glint of gold in its centre.

There was a terrible cry, a noise like a fist pounding on foam rubber, and with a sound of thunder Mr. Joshua Shepherd fell backward on to the pavement, the bullet head sunk up to its ears in his watch-draped abdomen.

*

Sergeant Giblet was a modern policeman. No gruff orders or oaths issued from his prim lips. When he spoke his voice was beautifully modulated and almost donnish in its accentuation. His free evenings were not spent idly about the dart-board in the Hare and Hounds, but as a leading figure in the local dramatic club. In his room, the white oak bookcase was filled with brightly jacketed words dealing with the scientific deduction of crime, and the psychology of criminals. He was very keen on self-improvement, but at the moment, none of his assets stood him in good stead.

With an air of acute embarrassment he turned away from the scowling face of the culprit to the thin girl who bent over the arm-chair, where reposed the groaning figure of the shop-keeper.

'Well, Officer, aren't you going to arrest him?' Harriet's voice was like sour cider. 'I quite clearly saw him take a pair of socks from the counter and hide them in his jacket. You saw them, didn't you? Then this terrible assault on poor Mr. Shepherd ; I suppose you know your duty, Officer.'

He ignored her and spoke to the store owner.

'It's up to you, sir,' he said coldly. 'The young lady is right in a sense, but it is up to you to make a formal charge, before I take him to the station. Actually I think we ought to make a few more inquiries first. After all, we know nothing about the boy, he hasn't even told us his name or where he lives yet. Still, of course if you say so we must arrest him right away.'

Mr. Shepherd was not at bottom a hard man, but he was a very injured one. His back still ached, where it had collided with the pavement. His stomach was still painful, but above all his vanity throbbed like a rotten tooth. He opened his mouth, began to bark out an order that the boy should be charged forthwith, and then paused.

His vanity had been hurt. Very much hurt. He had heard laughter as he had fallen. But, always the big but, how much more hurt would it be if he made a charge?

In the back of his mind he saw the headlines of the local press, heard the whispers of contempt, the fingers pointed at the man who had charged a child.

But, again the big but. If he was lenient. If he forgave completely, how different those headlines, those whispers could be.

' "Forgive us our trespasses," says store owner.' ' "The quality of mercy is not strained," says local J.P.' ' "Suffer little children," says Councillor Shepherd.'

'No, officer,' he said quietly, 'I don't think there is any need to charge the lad. I think he knows he's done wrong. If he tells us who he is and where he comes from, I don't think there is any need for a formal charge now, but I think you must see the parents.'

'Very good, sir.' Giblet was plainly relieved. 'Now, my boy, you've heard what the gentleman has said. He's very kindly offered to let you off, but you must tell us your name and where you live.'

'Orl right, mister, I'll tell you, me name's Bobbie Baker, and I live at Holyford.'

'I see.' Giblet wrote quickly in his notebook. 'Now Bobbie, why did you take those things from Mr. Shepherd's shop? Don't you know it is very wrong to take things that don't belong to you? Very wrong indeed.'

Bobbie spoke very slowly and carefully as if he were addressing a person of less than normal intelligence.

'Why did I come? 'Cos I had to come, of course. There was nobody else could get. Dad said somebody had to come, and as the others were all busy it 'ad to be me. Dad said it would be easy, it always was easy for me Ma on Wednesdays. It would 'ave been orl rite this time too if it hadn't been for 'er sticking 'er long nose in.' He darted a wicked glance at Harriet.

'Just a minute, just a minute.' All Mr. Shepherd's indignation was coming back, and he was beginning to regret the quality of mercy. 'You mean to tell me that your father sent you out to steal, that your mother was in the habit of stealing from my shop? That she made a practice of it, my boy?'

'Orl rite, mister, not so much of the boy, I've told you me name, you can use it, can't you? Ma come every Wednesday for the shopping. She couldn't come today, 'cos she's ill, so dad sent me, and now I suppose I've made a mess of it.' For the first time the voice sounded slightly tearful.

'Listen to me, Bobbie,' Harriet broke in. 'Is your mother a big woman with ginger hair, and does she wear a green dress?'

'That's rite, Miss, that's me Ma, lovely dress, ain't it, got it from Marks and Spencers, she did.'

'Very well, my boy, I think we'd better have a word with your father.' Giblet shut the notebook with an official snap.

'It's obviously a case of the home influence, sir. If you wouldn't mind I'd like you to come with us to the house, and you too, Miss. There's certain to be a charge against the parents.'

He put his hand on Bobbie Baker's fat shoulder and led him out to the waiting police car.

A mile or two to the east of the market town, the ground rises steeply, and then leaving the main land shelf pushes boldly out into the North Sea. At the end of this promontory lies Holyford.

Once, long ago, Holyford had been an important centre in the district.

A mound of overgrown ruins testifies to the presence of an abbey, founded by Irish monks in the ninth century, which had provided a flickering lamp of hope in the barren countryside. Pilgrims had come from all over Europe to visit the shrine of its founder, and once it is said a king had made the journey there, walking on bare and bleeding feet over the rough sea causeway to the abbey.

All the former glories had long since departed, however. The abbey is a mere mound, forgotten and weed-grown. Not more than a thousand souls live in the whole neighbourhood and it is doubtful if more than a handful of these remember a scrap of the local history.

The inhabitants of Holyford are a race apart from other men, for they do no work. A little fishing in the winter perhaps, but nothing at all regular. They have no arts, no local industry, they contribute nothing to the general good of the country and yet they live well and at peace ; for they have one asset more valuable than any district of England. They have no licensing laws.

Under a charter granted by that same barefooted king, no public house may be compelled to close its doors. A man may drink, and continue to drink there, and no one may be empowered to stop him. This charter has never been revoked, and so the inhabitants of this happy place remain prosperous.

No slump ever hits them. Year in, year out the shiny cars roll over the hills to their sanctuary. Every evening till late into the night, the six pubs resound with the laughter of the stock-brokers and city magnates who sit in their snug parlours, dispensing hospitality and largesse to the inhabitants, and paying heavily for the privilege.

As they approached the village, the expression of four of the five occupants of the car grew grimmer and grimmer.

To the police officers, Holyford was a dreadful nuisance, and a thorn in the side of law and order. To Harriet and Mr. Shepherd it was an abomination, a disgrace to the neighbour-hood, a veritable Gomorrah in their midst. They pursed their lips as the car rattled down the steep cobbled street, noting the roaring trade which was already being done by the 'Cross Keys', the 'Schooner', and the 'English Bowman'.

The Bakers' cottage stood at the end of the village, almost by the ramshackle, disused jetty. It was painted a brilliant white and looked like a railway poster.

They walked through the little garden, bright with geran-iums, and the Sergeant lifted the gleaming brass knocker, which Mr. Shepherd recognized as a best selling line from his hardware counter.

After a moment the door opened cautiously, and a round and very red face looked out. With a sudden movement, Bobbie tore himself from Giblet's grasp and ran to the owner of the face.

'Pa,' he cried, 'they got me, Pa, I couldn't help it, Pa, and they been treatin' me cruel. He dodged through into the cottage.

The red face's mouth dropped open like a trap door. For a moment he stared at them speechless, and then nodded.

'Orl right, officer. I suppose it's a fair cop. You mustn't blame the nipper though. It was me what put 'im up to it. Come inside, please, gentlemen, and you too, Miss, and I'll tell you 'ow it is.'

The inside of the cottage was as spotless as the exterior. From every corner of the room, china and brass ornaments winked at them.

Mr. Baker crossed to a plate silver box and took out a cigarette.

'I suppose there's no hobjection in me having a last one, superintendent,' he said to Giblet. 'I'll come quietly, I promise you. But it's the first time it's ever 'appened. I dunno what come over me sending the boy out to steal like that. I knew it

110

was wrong, of course, but then it's 'ard, sir, very 'ard for a poor man with a sick wife and three nippers to look after, no penshun either.'

'I see, Mr. Baker.' The notebook leapt to Giblet's hand like a conjuring trick. His Oxford accent seemed absurd in the cottage.

'I see, then you admit that you deliberately sent this child out to steal from Mr. Shepherd's store. Is that right?'

'Quite right, Superintendent, I did, I take full responsibility for everything. It's my fault.' He turned abjectly to Mr. Shepherd.

'You see, sir, with me wife ill, and the kids wanting so much I'adn't the strength to resist temptation. I'd a gone meself, sir, if I'd been a well man.

'Give us a chance, sir, the shame'll kill 'is mother. It's the first time any of us 'ave been in trouble. We'll make it up to you, sir.'

Harriet looked across at Shepherd's heavy face, and with disgust saw it begin to weaken.

'Just a moment, Mr. Baker,' she said coldly. 'I don't think that's true. Your wife may be ill. This may be the first time that the boy has been stealing, but I think your family have been taking things from the store for a long time. I think nearly everything you have here has been stolen. Isn't that true, Mr. Baker?'

'Why, you rotten, bloody, dried-up bitch.' Baker suddenly dropped all pathos and was tough and menacing. He leaned across the table and his hands worked together as if they longed to go around her throat. 'I'll teach you to speak about me family, about me pore sick wife like that.'

'All right, my man. That's enough of that, quite enough.' Giblet's hand was on his arm.

'I'm taking you along in a minute, but before I do I want a word with your wife, sick or not. Now where is she? Come on, Baker, where is she, out with it.'

With the question, all fight went out of Mr. Baker. He looked dumbly at the policeman, and then pointed to a door in the corner.

'She's in there, sir. But you can't go in. She won't let anybody in. Been a week in there, sir, locked the door and put a chair against it. Dunno what's wrong with 'er either. No food, not speaking to us at all, except to tell us to leave 'er alone. Over a week she's been in there, sir.'

'But what do you mean, over a week? Hasn't a doctor been to see her then?'

'No, Superintendent, never did 'old with doctors. She'll be

111

orl rite in a few days, I expect, if she's left alone, quiet like.'

'You mean to tell me that you've got a sick woman in there, whom you haven't seen or spoken to for seven days, and she's had no medical attention whatsoever?'

Giblet tried the door and then shouted.

'Mrs. Baker, I am a police officer. I have to speak to you. Will you please open the door at once.'

No reply came from within, but there was a noise of slightly moving bed springs.

'Mrs. Baker,' he called again. 'If you do not open the door I will have to break it in.' He motioned to the constable.

'Just a moment, officer.' Shepherd spoke hurriedly. 'Before you do that, before you break the door, oughtn't we to have a doctor here? I mean the shock, perhaps.'

'I don't really think the woman is sick at all, but just in case, I think you ought to fetch a doctor.'

'Yes, sir, I suppose you're right. Now, Baker, you may not hold with them, but all the same, you must know where the nearest doctor lives.'

'Nearest doctor.' Baker scratched his head. 'That'll be old Jacques. Not that he'll be much use to anybody. You'll find him in the "Keys" about now, I shouldn't wonder.'

'Right. Constable, run round to the "Cross Keys" and see if Dr. Jacques is there. If he is, ask him to step round here for a moment. Tell him that it is urgent.'

As they waited for the doctor, Harriet looked round the room and tried to take in its atmosphere.

It was clean and bright and fresh with flowers, but beneath all this she sensed something else.

Behind the polish and the smell of geraniums there was something else. Something stale and rotten and also sweet. Something that seemed to have been shut away for a long time was in the house with them. Something that was waiting to come out into the light. Something that horrified her. There was a terrible sense of relief as the door opened and a little, bald-headed, fussy man strode into the room.

Dr. Jacques was rarely annoyed, but he was always irritable. At the moment, he was very irritable indeed.

He had been taken away from a pleasant game of darts and a glass of bitter, and had been informed that he was to come at once to see Mrs. Baker, who was in some kind of legal trouble, and was probably feigning illness.

The Bakers were not patients of his, but they were in a way his friends; nearly everyone on the peninsula was his friend. Also he disliked policemen, and he meant to show it.

112

'Well, Sergeant, this is all most irregular. What is it? What can I do for you?' He turned from him to Baker.

'Hullo, Bert. Something the matter with the Missus, is there? Must be serious for me to be brought in. What's wrong with her? Now, Officer—' He drew himself up to his full, small height and thrust his turkey cock face up at Giblet.

When the matter had been explained to him, he was still not very impressed. He was the local G.P. of one of the most delinquent areas of England, and the shortcomings of his neighbours meant little to him. Probably old Ma Baker was a shop lifter and was shamming, but all the same he didn't see why he should be expected to act as a kind of unpaid detective.

Still, he supposed he'd better see her, she might just be ill, and there was that circular he'd had a few days ago, about reporting any unknown complaints. Where was it from? Yes, that la de da place Farhill, damned piece of impertinence. Even so, he'd have a look at her.

He turned away from the Sergeant to Baker.

'Well, Bert,' he said, and his voice was suddenly authoritative. 'What's the matter with her, what did she complain of?'

'Well, you see, doctor, we don't rightly know.' He scratched his head. 'It's like this. She said she 'ad toothache, awful swelling in 'er face there was, and she'd go and lie down for a bit. It's bin like that for a week, doctor. Locked the door, she did, kept saying she'd be orl right if only we left 'er alone. I sent the kids round to me sister's, and I been sleeping in the chair there.'

'I see, I see, well, are the rest of you all right?' He moved across the room to the cowering figure of Bobbie and tilted up his chin.

'Open your mouth, boy, and say ah. Keep still now. Well, there's nothing much the matter there, though those tonsils will have to come out soon.'

'Now, Sergeant, we medical chaps are wonderful fellows, you know. You'd be surprised at all the clever things they teach us at those colleges we went to. A real fund of knowledge we are. Practically nothing we can't do. But there is one thing, I'm afraid, and that is examining a sick person from behind a locked door. Have you got any suggestions, Sergeant, as to how it might be done?'

'Very good, sir.' Giblet moved back. 'Right oh, constable, we'll take it together.'

The two policemen stood together, and at Giblet's signal rushed at the door. They reached it shoulder to shoulder at exactly the right position of leverage. The door seemed to bend inward, there was a noise of tearing, straining wood and metal.

The hinges heaved against the post, heaved, tore again, and held.

As Harriet watched them walk back for a second attempt, she was suddenly afraid. As the crash of wood had sounded from the door, she had heard another sound behind it. A sound of something moving and something crying out. A moaning sound had been made behind the door. And yet not a moan, not anything associated with pain or sickness, but far stronger; it had been almost as if an animal was snarling to itself behind the closed door.

'Ready, constable, right, together now. One, two, three.' Side by side the two men hurled themselves again at the door. Once more it seemed to hold, then the screws were torn out of the wood and it swung open.

It was very dark inside the room. The small window at the back was tightly shuttered and no light could have penetrated for days. From the open doorway a thin pencil of sunlight pointed like a flash lamp into the darkness.

It waved into that room, clean and bright, and all the colours of the rainbow were in its narrow beam. Harriet looked along it as it wavered round the closed room. It picked out the table, a chair, the frilly lace curtains of the window, and finally rested upon the end of the heavy brass bedstead, which shone like gold in its light. And then suddenly the bed was gone. It was gone because something had taken its place. Something had moved in front of it into the sunlight.

For a fraction of a second Harriet looked at the something, and then she covered her eyes. She covered her eyes and didn't look any more. She didn't think any more. She couldn't even scream any more, but clawed her way blindly across the Bakers' trim parlour, searching desperately for the front door, as she fled from the mutant that was standing in the dark bedroom.

CHAPTER THIRTEEN

At last the sun had left England, and the sky was very, very grey. Far below them, the Holyford peninsula pushed out into the water like a green worm in the sea; specks of white breaking lazily upon its flanks.

They were dropping down to it now. The sound of the propeller had changed and they were sinking through the grey sky as through a lift shaft. Houses, trees, human beings were rushing up to meet them, as the landscape details shot into view. Then the plane seemed to pull upwards again, hang motionless, and fall as softly as thistledown on to the grass, before the square red buildings that could only be the Holyford Cottage Hospital.

Tony grinned and nodded to the pilot, and got out. There was no one to meet him. A group of villagers stared incredulously at the helicopter, but there was no sign of anybody in authority.

He walked across the grass and up the marble steps, past a bronze plaque, bearing a list of the founder's virtues, and into the gleaming hall.

The hall was empty. He peered into the deserted reception desk, banged the bell, and waited. Nobody came, but from a door at the end of the hall he heard voices and a sound as of somebody sobbing.

He walked over to the door, knocked on it, and went into the room. It was full of women.

At least twelve nurses were wedged into that small room, gathered around a thin young probationer, who sat on a chair, rocking backwards and forwards, sobbing as if her heart was breaking.

For a moment nobody noticed Tony and then one of them, wearing a sister's uniform, turned and looked at him.

'Oh, I'm very sorry, but I'm afraid that this room is strictly private. Did you want to see someone?'

'Yes, Sister, where can I find Dr. Jacques?'

'Dr. Jacques, I'm afraid that is impossible just now. Doctor is very busy, perhaps I can take a message for you?'

'No message, Sister, but I think he'll see me at once. I have an appointment with him. My name is Heath, from Farhill.'

'Of course, Mr. Heath; yes, Doctor has been expecting you.' Her voice was full of relief. 'Doctor and Matron are with the patient, I'll take you to them at once.'

'One moment, Sister.' Tony's heart beat a little faster with her words. 'You mean your matron is with the case which was admitted today? Didn't you have instructions that the patient was to be placed in the strictest isolation?'

'Oh yes, we did, but Doctor didn't think it meant staff. Besides only Doctor and Matron have been near her since she was brought in. And of course Nurse Pattison.' She pointed to the crying figure on the chair.

'I see, well it's probably too late now, in any case. Sister, will you please show me where I can find the patient, and then I want you to place Nurse Pattison in a private ward by herself. Nobody is to go near her for the time being. No, I don't want

115

any arguments, Sister, just do what I tell you and show me where Doctor Jacques is.'

She led him out into the hall, pointed to a corridor and then went back to the group of nurses.

Tony walked across the hall to the passage, the steel heels of his shoes clicking like marbles on the polished floor. At the end of the corridor there was a door. He went through it, and crossed the little ward to a bed. There was a tall woman at the foot of the bed, and a little man who reeked of whisky. Tony ignored them and bent over the bed.

And there was no doubt, no shadow of doubt. It had come to England. From the white pillows the same face looked up at him as it had done from the Russian refrigerator. But if the first thing had been a nightmare, this was part of hell itself, for it was alive.

For not more than three seconds did Tony glance at the strapped creature on the bed, and then he turned to the man beside him.

'Dr. Jacques, I'm Heath from Farhill. We must get out of here at once.' Jacques nodded and obeyed blindly like a child; he was obviously very near breakdown.

In the passage he clutched Tony's arm.

'Mr. Heath, what is it, tell me quickly, what is it? I've never seen anything like it.'

'Sorry, doctor, not now; there's no time for any explanation at the moment, we've work to do. You all right, Matron?'

She nodded briefly. She was firm and Scotch and her face was lined with the honourable lines of duty and fortitude.

'Yes, I'm all right, thank you. I'll just sit down for a minute and perhaps have a cup of—'

'No, I'm sorry. Matron, before you do that you must do something for me first. One of your nurses, Nurse Pattison, has been put into a private ward. I want you to go and stay with her for the time being.'

'I see, Mr. Heath, what you mean is that we're both potential carriers, that we may be infected. That's it, isn't it?'

Before he could answer her, she turned away and walked stiffly and fearlessly down the corridor.

In his office, Jacques motioned Tony to a seat and then, without speaking, crossed to a cupboard. He took a tube from a shelf and with a quick motion swallowed two green capsules. When he turned round a moment later, his face looked firmer, more reliant.

'Ah, that's better, much better. Now, Mr. Heath, tell me about it, what is it?'

'No, I'm still sorry, doctor, but there is not time for an

116

explanation at the moment. But you must believe me when I tell you that that thing you have in there has the power to destroy the human race in a matter of months.'

Jacques nodded. 'Yes, I believe you,' he said. 'But what do we do? What is the treatment?'

'There's no treatment at the moment, doctor, no hope of a cure. All we can hope for is the prevention of an outbreak.'

'I see, then when you say isolation—'

'When I say isolation, I mean utter and complete isolation. That room must be sealed. The doors and the windows must be made air-tight, and when that is done, nobody must go near that part of the hospital.'

'But Mr. Heath, I can't do that. That would be murder. I'm only a local G.P. you know, not a very good one, perhaps. I drink far too much, but I still remember my oath, my duty. My place is with my patient, whatever the risk.'

'Dr. Jacques.' Tony' voice was very weary. 'I'm sure you're a very good doctor, but you must do as I say. You don't understand, doctor. You have no patient. There is no woman in there, nothing that you could call a woman, a human being. All humanity has gone. That creature, although it has a basic human form and probably still retains some traces of a thought process, is no more human than—than a piece of grass by the roadside.

'The spores that have changed her into that are a man-made mutation, and they are more active, more deadly, more voracious, than anything mankind has yet experienced. I beg you to believe me and carry out my instructions. I'll take full responsibility for them.'

For a moment Jacques was silent. He tapped his pencil on the desk and then, as if coming to a sudden decision, picked up the house phone and gave a series of curt orders.

'Well, that's done. I've told the porters to have the door and the windows sealed and the staff to keep out of that wing. And may God forgive me. Now what?'

'Thank you, doctor; now I want to know exactly what persons have been in contact with the case during the last six days, that is vital.'

'Yes, yes, of course, I've got it here.' Jacques took a notebook out of his desk and flicked through it. 'Here we are.'

'The husband stated that she had been alone in that room for seven days, seeing nobody. That may seem strange to you, leaving her alone for that period, but they're strange people round here, and I'm quite prepared to believe him.

'They would look at it like this. They heard her moving about, she asked them to leave her alone, so they would do so.

She would probably recover all right, and if she didn't, well, no damned quack could help her.

'That means that the only direct contacts have been, let me see, the husband, myself, Matron, Nurse Pattison, the two police officers, and the boy, Bobbie. Oh yes, and there was that chap Shepherd and his assistant.'

'I see.' Tony thought for a moment. 'That means that we have nine definite and recent contacts, and probably others, if she had been in that room for seven days. A room with a door that doubtless didn't fit.' Helplessness was running through him like water. Nine definite contacts. Still he had to go on. However slight a hope there was.

'Now, doctor, you're here. The matron and the nurse are in a private ward. Where are the others?'

'I'm afraid I don't really know. Baker and the boy were taken to the police station, I believe. Shepherd and Miss Soper will have probably gone back to town by now, I suppose.'

Tony put his hand to his forehead. It was too late, they had lost. They had lost because of the secrecy imposed on them by a government that feared civic unrest more than death. If the country had been warned of what to expect before the attack, they might have had a chance, but now! Still, he had to keep on fighting. Whatever the odds, he had to go on fighting.

'Now, doctor, I'm sorry, but I must take charge from now on. I want you to consider yourself in quarantine for the present. I have to leave you now. I must make an examination of the—the patient, and then I have to see the Chief Constable; I understand he lives near here.'

Jacques started to protest and then stopped. The young man impressed him terribly and his word was backed up by what he had seen.

'The Chief Constable? Yes, of course, Colonel Briggs, very difficult man, very difficult indeed, lives in a big, red house just at the bottom of the slope. You can't miss it. Yes, good-bye for the time being, Mr. Heath.'

He made a gesture of resignation and watched Tony walk out of the room.

He sat still in his chair for a time, and then pulled open a drawer and placed a tall, amber bottle on the desk before him.

*

Colonel Briggs was tall and spare and his face was tanned more by spirits than sun and wind.

He stood against the mantelpiece of the gloomy, trophy-hung cage he called his den, and frowned at Tony.

118

'No more, Mr. Heath, please no more. Quite enough—don't understand technical matters—don't want to—never did—can't help it—one of those things.' He drew heavily at a stale, rank pipe.

'Now, Mr. Heath. What you've told me makes a very nasty picture—very nasty indeed. But what can I do—don't doubt your word—far from it—seen your credentials, but I ask you, what can I do? Got a bit of power here—not much—very little really. What you want me to do is much more than that power allows. Seal an area—lock up a number of people—all because of what you've told me—can't do it—like to help—sorry—but just can't. Have to send in full report to Home Office—get their permission—take time, yer know—lot of time—slow moving fellers up there—very slow.

'What I don't get is this. If so urgent, why wasn't I informed before about it—should have been, you know—might have done something then—don't know, but might have.'

'Colonel Briggs.' Tony almost grovelled before the man. 'You were not told, because we didn't for one minute imagine it would reach us so soon. The Government wouldn't let us give details to anyone outside our department, because they feared disturbances. But now you must take my word for it. You must do what I say.'

'What's that! Must? Now look here, young feller me lad. As I said, I don't doubt your credentials—not for a minute—far from it—like to help—sure you technical chaps know what you're up to, but try and see my point for a bit. You come in here—tell me some kind of plague has broken out in the village —area to be sealed off—fellow put into quarantine. I ask you? Home Office knows nothing about it—Lord Lieutenant knows nothing about it—not that he knows much about anything these days, but I ask you, what can I do?'

'Colonel, I quite see your point, I quite see how difficult this is for you, but if you'd just ring up this number, it's General Kirk at Foreign Office Intelligence, I'm sure he'd be able to persuade you.' He felt sticky with the effort of pleading with the man.

'What's that—Intelligence, where do they come in? Spies and things, that's their line, ain't it? No, the Home Office is my master. Just a minute though. What name did you say? Kirk. Not Hookey Kirk feller who used to be in the brigade? Is it Hookey you mean?'

'I don't know, sir. General Kirk is in charge of this matter.'

'Fat feller, about sixty I should say—got two fingers on one hand—right hand I think—lost others at Wipers—that the man?'

Tony nodded, and with relief watched Briggs reach for the telephone; it seemed that social contact was going to work where he had failed. It was ages before the Colonel was connected and ages before he was put through to Kirk. Then things began to move very quickly. Briggs's gruff inquiries into the General's health were roughly thrust aside and he listened meekly to the voice at the end of the line. His face was darker than normal when he replaced the instrument.

'Phew! that was Hookey all right. Hasn't altered a bit, always a martinet.

'Why didn't you tell me before, young feller—I do what Hookey tells me—when Kirk says turn we all turn, eh. Well, come on, my boy, we mustn't hang about here when there's work to do. We'd better get down to the police station and give those idle fellers there something to think about.'

At the local police headquarters it was apparent that Briggs's powers were not as limited as he had made out.

After a few curt orders the powers that be fairly leapt into activity. Squads of police cars were brought in from the rest of the county, and a cordon was drawn across the neck of the peninsula. Ambulances raced through the streets picking up all the known contacts, and by the evening Tony felt he could relax for a moment. He had at last screened the area for the time being. The matter was for the moment in Briggs's hands.

As dusk slowly crept in from the sea, two bright spears of light crossed and recrossed the narrow neck of land. They were the two searchlights which had been put there to light up every detail of the landscape to the patrolling police. No one could leave the peninsula that night.

Tony looked at them and listened to the harsh tones of the loudspeakers telling the inhabitants to keep calm.

'Keep calm, this was merely a temporary emergency, it was quite in hand, everything was all right. There was no cause for alarm. They would be all right, if they didn't panic and kept calm. That was all they had to do. Keep calm and trust the authorities.'

'Trust the authorities.' Tony shivered. What authorities? Trust him. Trust Kirk and Hearn. Trust the Russians who had lost the north of their country by now. Trust who else?

How long was it now? Five days, only five days since he had been sitting in his study in Durford feeling listless and bored and longing for a change. Well, he had the change all right now. England had the change, the world had the change.

How long ago was it since a Russian biologist had first stood as he was standing looking at a cordoned area and wondering when they would have to move back again? How long?

120

He turned as Briggs came towards him, through the twilight, as stiff and straight as a ramrod.

'Ah, there you are, old man. Well, I think things are settled down a bit now. At first I thought we were going to have a spot o' bother. Nearly a riot on our hands for a bit. Still, all right now. All quiet and peaceful; don't know for how long though. How's your end going now? Got all your quarantine people locked up all right?'

'Yes, I think so. All the known contacts, anyway.'

'Good, now where do we go from here? How long do we have to keep the place cut off? How long before you people get it cleared up? Let's go into the super's office for a while. The Home Office want a full verbal report from me in the morning, so perhaps you can put me into the picture a bit more. None of your technical jargon though.'

After Tony had talked for a few minutes, the lean, tanned face seemed to go soft and puffy. His well manicured hands shook as they filled the pipe and his voice was the voice of an old tired man.

'I see, so that's it, is it. Please forgive me for not believing you at first, Just an old fossil at times, I'm afraid. And it only attacks women, and you don't know how to stop it. God! the devil, the filthy, bloody, unprintable devil.

'So, we just have to wait and hope that your friend Hearn is able to find a cure, or that old Kirk can get his hands on that bitch. What's her name? Yes, Steinberg. And if he doesn't, we just move back again. Well, one thing, thank God I'm not married.

'Oh! my dear chap, I'm terribly sorry. You are, aren't you? I really am sorry. Please forgive me. Just an old fossil, as I said.' His voice was full of concern.

'It's quite all right, Colonel, there's nothing to forgive, you weren't to know. How could you? But I think if you don't mind I'll just ring up my wife. May I use your phone?'

'My dear boy, of course. Take this one. I'll leave you alone for a bit, I want to have a word with the inspector, in any case. With a grunt he heaved himself out of his seat and strode briskly to the door.

Tony hesitated for a moment and then dialled the Farhill number. They were a long time putting him through and as he waited he almost began to dread speaking to Marcia.

He pictured her in the little antiseptic bedroom at the top of the huge building, waiting for him to phone and the very thought of her existence filled him with despair.

Why was she alive, why did she exist at all? Exist in the same world as that. He thought of the thing in the sealed room behind the searchlights. The thing that fought with its no flesh against the straps that held it and had mouthed at him with its no mouth as he bent over it. And he thought of his wife's sweet flesh.

He thought of the thing with its grey-green hair which was not hair, and he thought of her dark auburn hair, the hair of her head and the hair of her body.

He thought of her face, and the way the nose crinkled when she smiled, and the curve of her lips and the curve of her breasts, and the way she laughed when they came from the opera. The way she laughed when they came home from the opera and walked back to her blue room in the evening. The scarf tied over the light bulb, and the bed, dark like an oasis in the city. The sun coming up over her face in the morning and her hair spread on the pillow like rain. She was all he had, all he needed, and yet he dreaded the reminders of her soft body.

His eyes were smarting as the click came at the end of the line, and a voice spoke to him.

He waited for a second for the lump in his throat to clear and then asked for Hearn.

When he heard the big man's voice he felt better.

Alone in this bleak, disease-ridden countryside he had felt terribly cut off and helpless. A mere spectator divorced from the real battle, merely waiting for it to happen.

Hearn's voice brought back his confidence. In the laboratory and in Kirk's office they were fighting this thing. Soon they would destroy it. Soon they would have something. Soon Kirk would tell them what they had to know.

For the third time that day, he spoke to the director, going over the details again, giving him every scrap of information he had been able to gather.

He could hear Hearn grunting from time to time, and could visualize his huge hand scrawling notes on his pad.

'I see, then you've been through all the contacts and there don't seem to be any more cases at the moment? Good boy. Now there is nothing else, is there?'

'No, I don't think so. I think I've given you everything there is. There's one thing though. It's only to be expected in a way, and it won't help you at all, but the smell of the creature. Most peculiar. Not fungoid at all. Rather like, how shall I put it, new-mown hay.'

Hearn paused as he took this down.

'Really, how extraordinary. Smells like new-mown hay. Thank you. Well, Tony, let me know if there are any further developments. Hang on now. I think your wife wants to speak to you.'

He waited for her, and his hand was sticky round the phone. When she spoke it was as if they were in the same room together. For a few seconds he listened to her calm, unfrightened voice and then started to speak very slowly and firmly to her.

'Listen, darling. I want you to listen to me and do just what I tell you. Just this once, exactly what I tell you without any argument or question.

'I think everything is going to be all right. Kirk has promised us the details of the radiations, as you know, and when we get them we're going to wipe this thing off the face of the map. That's quite definite.'

He lied plausibly to her, and for a split second to himself.

'Now, darling, until we know exactly how long this is going to take and exactly what the danger is I want you to do something for me. I want you to leave Farhill in the morning. It's no place for you. I want you to go down to North Wales for a day or two. George and Joan will be so glad to have you. Ring them up in the morning and go straight down. Don't tell them anything, just say that you felt like a change.

'Now, darling, don't argue. I'm perfectly all right, so just this once don't argue. I'll ring you in Wales tomorrow evening.

'Good-night, my darling, good-night, my lovely darling.'

Before she could reply, he put down the receiver.

*

In the morning the clouds had cleared away and the sun rose bright and brilliant over the peninsula.

It lit up the grey water and the rocky coastline, and the roofs of the houses.

It shone on the faces of the police as they stood watching the roads, haggard with their night's vigil, and the irate, puzzled villagers as they prepared for another day cut off from the mainland.

Farther south, it beat on the closed windows of Kirk's stifling office, and the Farhill laboratory where Hearn bent over the test tubes.

It shone on the graceful façade of a Georgian house where a dying man was trying to reach a decision, and the dim panes of Briggs's gloomy study.

There was only one place where it failed to gain entrance. A small hospital room, screened from sun and air by heavy plastic sheeting. A room in which something fought and struggled against the straps that held it to the bed.

A room that smelt strangely of new-mown hay.

CHAPTER FOURTEEN

MARCIA never had the slightest idea of disobeying Tony. She had sensed the near breaking point in his voice when she had listened to him on the phone, and she certainly did not intend to add to his worries by any refusal.

She hated the idea of going to Wales though. Hated the thought of being left out of things, of being cut off, of not knowing what was happening. Still, if that was what he wanted she would go.

She threw the few things that she had brought from Durford into a case and went down to the hall. There was a train directory in the porter's office. She asked for it and began to look up a train to Chester.

It was then that she got the idea. It was a trivial idea. In a way an obvious idea, but it was very nearly going to cost her her life. She had plenty of time, it was only just after eight o'clock. She had all day to get there and her suitcase felt pitifully light.

Joan would be pleased to lend her some things, of course, but why should she bother her?

She thought of her well-stocked drawers at home, and at once looked up the trains to and from Durford.

Yes, she could do it easily. She had plenty of time to go home, collect some more clothes, and get a train which would be in Wales in time for dinner.

She had half an hour to get to King's Cross. Not long enough to phone her friends, so she scribbled a note, asked the porter to send a telegram for her, and running out of the building, past the grinning security guards, hurled herself into a taxi. She only just made it. The big clock in the tower showed seconds to spare as they pulled into the station.

She almost threw the money at her driver, fought her way through the milling city crowds, and promising to pay the collector, pushed past the barrier as the long train drew out of the station. The compartment was hot and dirty and full of grit, the window wouldn't open, but it had one great advantage. It was nearly empty.

Nearly, but not quite. In the corner by the door sat a large,

124

red-faced woman with a huge luncheon basket on her knees. She grinned broadly as Marcia pulled herself into the moving train and chuckled sympathetically.

'Just made it, my dear, just made it,' she said.

'You want to be careful though. They say they've had some terrible accidents with people doing that. Dreadful things, these trains. When you're late they start on time, and when you're early, they dawdle about in the station for hours. Just like everything these days, terrible, really. I was just going to have a bite to eat, my dear, when you came in. Didn't have any time for breakfast. Perhaps you'll join me? Yes, do, there's plenty for both of us.'

Marcia had to make a quick decision. She hadn't eaten for hours and she was desperately hungry. Yet she would have to pay for her breakfast, she was quite sure of that. Something in the large lady's eyes told her that she would have to pay, if not in cash at least in something else. In conversation.

Still, she was hungry and the aroma of coffee was very strong. She accepted the invitation, and together they fell on the basket as the train clattered and groaned through the northern tunnels.

Mrs. Coffin, for that was the large lady's name, was looking forward to an enjoyable journey. She loved a good chat, and in particular, a chat with a stranger.

A stranger could never stop her. A stranger could never say that such and such a story had been told before. She didn't need to think which of the exploits of the Coffin family she had already recounted, but could let things flow quite naturally. And Marcia was just the kind of person she liked talking to. Young, pretty, if a little pale and tired looking. Very much the lady. Exactly what she wanted.

So Mrs. Coffin talked. She talked of her large family. Her husband and his many ailments. A recent visit to her married daughter in Kent, and the failings of her son-in-law. She talked of her two sons, their jobs, their motor-cycles, and their girl friends. She talked and talked. She talked through Hatfield and Peterborough. Through Retford and Newark. She talked on and on. By Grantham she appeared to have exhausted the topic of her family for a moment and turned to life in general. The pleasures of chance meetings with strangers in trains, for example. How often such contacts could lead to more. How deep friendships could be built up in this way.

'Take you and me, dear, I've so enjoyed our little chat, and I do hope we can keep in touch with each other, but if you think about it, it's a hundred to one we'd have met in a social way before.'

'Yes, yes, I'm sure you're right,' said Marcia, who hadn't spoken for over half an hour, then not wishing to appear rude.

'I'm afraid I'm not very good company this morning, it's just that I'm awfully tired.'

'Tired, yes I thought you were, dear. You were almost dropping off just now, didn't you feel me shaking you?' She completely missed Marcia's glance of fury at this information.

'The trouble with you young people is the hours you keep. Early to bed, early to rise, that's my motto. And you smoke too much, you know, dear. Why, you must have had six or seven once we left London. It doesn't do you any good, you know.

'I never let any of my daughters start to smoke when they were young, and I'm glad to say none of them do now. Much better for it. My old man now, always at it. Like a blooming great kid with a dummy, he is. Said he couldn't afford it a while back and started growing his own. Awful stuff, worse than before. My Ethel said—but I haven't told you about Ethel yet, have I?'

So she told her. She told her about Ethel, who had started as an infant prodigy and had apparently never looked back.

Marcia was taken through Ethel's infancy, her schooldays, and the glowing reports. Her brilliance at college. Her service as a nurse.

'Wonderful Ethel was in the war. Sister before she had her twenty-first birthday. And do you know, at the end of the war —I shouldn't be telling you this really, dear, but I'm sure it won't go any farther. You know how the Government said they wouldn't send any of the girls to the front lines.

'Well, that wasn't true. They did send some of them to Germany, and my Ethel was one of them. Oh, I would have been worried if I'd known at the time. Just a few picked ones, of course. Terrible it was, she said. Why, they were right up behind the boys. One of them just disappeared. Walked out of her billet, and was never seen again. Awful shock it gave Ethel.

'Now, my Bert—'

Without check or remorse, the relentless voice droned on. The sun beat on the closed window, the flat, dull scenery rolled past them, the heat of the compartment was unbearable. And still the voice went on and on.

Marcia leaned against the grimy cushions and tried to endure it. She mustn't be rude, whatever happened, she mustn't be rude. Mrs. Coffin was fundamentally a nice creature, if a bore. She mustn't hurt her feelings.

She gritted her teeth and nodded and smiled politely at the streams of useless information that poured forth.

126

There was only one short respite. Having come to the end of one interminable story, Mrs. Coffin rose ponderously from the seat and, clutching her bag, moved swaying to the toilet.

For a moment, Marcia was able to close her eyes and relax, but only for a moment. The door was thrown open with a bang and a gruff official demanded her ticket.

By the time he had taken her fare and grumblingly written a receipt, Mrs. Coffin was back with her.

'Eh, I did get a shock, dear. I opened the door of the lav, and there was that guard standing right outside waiting for my ticket. The impertinence. A bit of tact, that's what some of these gentlemen want.

'Well, we must be getting near Durford now, I should think. You did say you were going to Durford, didn't you? Do you live there?'

'Oh no, no, I'm just visiting friends for a short time,' Marcia lied quickly, on the spur of the moment.

'Oh, what a pity, I was hoping we might have gone on seeing a bit of each other. What is your friends' name?'

'Their name, oh yes, Shakespere.'

'Shakespere, well, I've heard that name somewhere before, but I don't seem to place it. Whereabouts in Durford do they live?'

Her inquiries were mercifully cut short, as with a scream of brakes the train began to slow down.

Mrs. Coffin pulled an enormous suitcase down from the rack and adjusted her hat.

'Ah, well, dear, here we are. I've so much enjoyed meeting you and if you do have the time, come round and see us. We love having friends in and the tele's always on in the evening.'

'I'm so sorry,' said Marcia, 'I'd really like to, but I'm only staying a day or two.'

'What a shame. All the same, I'll give you the address and if you can manage it, you will come round, won't you?' She pulled a notebook out of her bulging bag and scribbled on a leaf, as the train drew into the station.

'That's it, my dear. It's got a phone number and all. Whatever I say about the old man, he's a good provider.' She handed the torn paper to Marcia.

'Here we are.' She lifted her case on to the floor and opened the door.

'Good-bye, dear, I've so much enjoyed talking to you. Do give me a ring and come round to see us if you can.'

She strode off manfully down the crowded platform, larger than life and completely self-confident.

Marcia checked the time of her connexion to Wales and looked at her watch.

She had exactly an hour to spare. Just nice time to go home, have a wash, pack a few things, and get back to the train. Yes, thank God, it had a dining car.

She walked briskly up the hill to the cathedral, and a few minutes later was opening the door of their little house.

Inside everything was exactly as it had been before. For a moment it seemed as if nothing had happened. All the past few days had been suddenly swept away.

Tony was upstairs preparing his lecture for the morning. The tea party had just finished. No door bell had rung for Hearn. Nothing at all had happened.

But it had. Somewhere to the north of her, Tony was struggling to check this outbreak in a cut-off, cordoned village.

The well-groomed, self-satisfied Dr. Hearn was a mere shadow of himself, as he stood in the Farhill laboratory, desperately waiting for the news that Kirk had promised him. And she—

She looked into the mirror and turned away from the sight of her pale, haggard face.

Still, there was no time for thinking about that. She ran upstairs and began to pack a large suitcase, putting all her best things in, for if you are going to die, at least you can die in your finest feathers.

When she came downstairs again she noted that she still had over half an hour to spare. She looked at the milk bottles on the step and put the kettle on. There was plenty of time for a cup of coffee.

She made it, carried the tray through into the sitting-room, and sat down. She was just about to put the cup to her lips when she noticed the book. It lay untidily at the end of the sofa where she had left it four days ago, and the bright dust jacket was visible. The cup shook in her hand and a few drops of coffee spilled on to her dress, as she stared at it.

It was a wartime novel about nurses, and the cover showed a blonde girl in a blue battledress leaning against the wall of a shed. There were rolls of barbed wire beside the shed and smoking shell craters in the background. But it wasn't the girl, or the craters, or the wire that was significant, it was the battledress that mattered. The well-cut feminine battledress that fitted her like a glove.

What was it Roberts had said about his interview with Steinberg?

'When I saw her they had put her into one of the sleeping

128

quarters of the hut. They had taken away her own clothes and she was wearing a battledress.'

And that was the difficulty, the one thing she couldn't understand about Steinberg's escape.

The fighting was over in the area. The countryside must have been swarming with refugees at that time. It would have been easy for an insignificant-looking woman to mingle with them But only if her dress was insignificant too.

A small woman dressed in a British soldier's battledress would stand out in any crowd of refugees. Every guard at every checkpoint would spot her. She wouldn't last five minutes. It was impossible.

But if, if it wasn't a soldier's battledress, if it was something else, something that fitted her. Then—

She rummaged in her bag and desperately searched for the scrap of paper that Mrs. Coffin had given her. She had put it away out of politeness, meaning to throw it away later, and mercifully it was still there. She unfolded it and reached for the phone.

A moment later she was listening to the voice that had bored her all the way from London.

'Mrs. Coffin, it's Marcia Heath speaking, Yes, Marcia Heath; we came up from London in the train together.'

For a moment the line was silent and then the voice leapt into action again. She waited for the torrent to stop, and then spoke very quietly and firmly into the phone.

'No, Mrs. Coffin, I'm afraid I can't get round to see you this time. It's about something else that I wanted to speak to you.

'You remember in the train how you were telling me about your daughter, Ethel I think you said her name was. Yes, that's right, the one who was a nurse.

'What I wanted to know was, does she live with you? She does, then I wonder if I could speak to her for a moment.'

There was a pause and then a very quiet, intelligent, and rather cultured voice was at the end of the line.

Marcia asked a question, and for a long time listened to the reply. Then she thanked the voice and put down the phone. She knew what she wanted. She looked at the rough notes she had scrawled on the blotter.

Yes, it was fitting together. It could have been done that way. Roberts's memory could have been correct. She could have been wearing a battledress and got away. But not a thick khaki battledress. Not a soldier's with unit tags.

No, a dark blue, nicely cut affair with red crosses on it. After all, a nurse could go anywhere. A nurse was international. And if that nurse had a patient with her—a patient who was suffer-

129

ing from paralysis, perhaps, or pretending to suffer from it. A man who was described as being on intimate terms with her, but who denied it. A man who had admitted to a friend that he knew where and how she had gone. A man with a rich woman in England who would do anything for him. Who would hide his friend if he asked her.

Yes, it all fitted together. The uniform. The long wait, while the forged papers were prepared. Then the crowded troopship. The guards unsuspicious of a uniform, and a Georgian house in the country. A Georgian house with a man sitting on a terrace and a nurse beside him. A nurse who got up and left as soon as a stranger appeared.

Yes, it could be that. It could be the way. And if it was, they had won. Steinberg was in their hands.

She looked at her watch. Her train would be in in five minutes, but it was no longer important. She had to prove her theory.

It was quite clear what she should do. She had the Farhill phone number in front of her. She had only to call Hearn and he would tell Kirk.

Still, after all it was only a hunch. True her first one about Steinberg had been right, but she had to check it. There was only one way. She must ask Roberts.

If Roberts said that it had been a nurse's blue battledress that Steinberg was wearing, her idea would be more than a theory. She must be sure of that before she bothered Kirk.

She put on her hat and went to the door.

Since she had got out of the train, the weather had been changing. There was a smell of rain in the air, and dark clouds were creeping towards the pallid sun that froze over the cathedral. It was a small watery sun, but she wished it would stay. She looked up at it for a moment, turned up her collar, and then walked down the hill.

The street was the same as she remembered it from that first visit. When Tony and she had called together on Roberts, it had been early morning and the district had seemed fresh and clean, but now, as on that first bright evening, it was stale and fly-blown.

She passed the same dismal bars, the grey mounds of tripe in the shop window, the scrawled messages and obscenities, the same grimy pointing children.

She hurried on past them and turned into the garden of the grim, oversized house.

Once more she pulled the rusty handle and once more a bell sounded, far away in the back.

'Please God he's in,' she thought. 'And if he's in, please God

130

he'll remember. Just let him remember, and let the answer be the one I want. If he gives me the right answer, everything will be all right. We'll have won, and everything will be all right again.

'If only I'm right, Kirk will pick her up today. He'll make her talk. He'll get the figures Tony and Hearn want. They'll work something out from those figures and then—then I can sleep again.

'So let him remember. Let him remember and tell me the battledress was blue. Oh God, let it be blue.'

Her heart beat wildly with excitement and hope as the door opened and Roberts peered out at her.

CHAPTER FIFTEEN

'YES, sir,' said Kirk into the telephone. 'It's time now, sir. Yes, I'm quite sure about that. You'll have to make an announcement now ...

'Yes, I'm certain we're going to have a lot of trouble. There are bound to be disturbances when they know, but things have gone too far for you to hold back any longer ...

'Yes, as far as we know, at the moment, things are in hand in the North. I've just heard from the man at Farhill a few minutes ago. There are no more suspected cases for the time being, but of course we can't be sure ...

'Yes, they did send out a circular to all area medical officers, but I think we need more than that now. As you know, this outbreak in England was much sooner than we thought. We believed we had another four days at least ...

'Of course they're doing all they can at Farhill, sir. As a matter of fact, I'm hoping we may break it by morning, but as there's so little time I do feel you must make it public as soon as possible ...

'I see. Good. All local authorities in the morning, then, and you'll make an announcement during the nine o'clock news. I'm certain you're doing the right thing, sir. Thank you very much. Good-bye.'

Well, so it had come to that. The public were to be told. Very much against his own wish, the advice of his ministers, and the American government, the Prime Minister was going to make it public. Tomorrow evening at nine o'clock he would get up before a microphone and tell the world what had happened.

No doubt he would offer hopes and assurances, but Kirk could still visualize the unrest and possibly panic that would ensue. Still, it had to be done. Whatever the consequences, it had to be done. Now that England was affected, the world had to be told.

He had the latest information from Russia on the desk before him. The area was still rolling back.

So far there were no reports of an outbreak elsewhere. Only England and Russia were affected.

That was strange, two countries so far apart, but it was not his job to wonder about it. His job was to get the figures Hearn needed, and then he would have finished.

He looked up at the clock on the wall. His cigar was cold between his lips as he watched the swift, jerking minute hand.

It was five thirty, there was half an hour to go. He had given Mrs. Haversfield till six o'clock to contact him, and the time was almost up. The sand was almost at the bottom of the glass. If she didn't come at six, his last trail would have died out. His last lead on Steinberg would have gone. There was no other hope left. It would be as if she had disappeared into the ground.

Loser would be put on to the night plane for East Germany, and when he went, Kirk's only remaining connexion with Ruhleben would have gone too.

There were twenty-five minutes of hope left. He started as the door opened and his secretary came in with a cup of tea.

He growled his thanks, forced himself to drink a little of the dark, leathery liquid, and looked up at her.

'You're sure everybody is clued up about this evening, Florrie? When Mrs. Haversfield gets here, I want her shown straight in to me. I want her fairly rushed up here as soon as she enters the building. No waiting or hanging about at all.

'When she leaves, I want her followed every inch of the way. Wherever she goes. Is that clear?'

'Yes, of course, General, everybody knows what to do. Now just take it easy. She'll come all right. I'm sure she will.' She beamed maternally at the man old enough to be her grandfather, picked up the tray, and swept out of the room.

*

It was two minutes to the hour when she came. She came into the room so silently that for a moment he didn't notice her. She stood looking at him, and she was as cold and self-

132

possessed as when he had first seen her. Only her eyes gave her away. He looked at the beautiful, ravaged face and then got up and motioned her to a seat.

'No thank you, General Kirk, I think I prefer to stand. Besides, what I have to say will not take long and I have not much time, I still have to pack his things, you see.'

'Ah, then he didn't tell you anything. May I?' he motioned to his cigar.

'Of course.' She waited for him to light it and then went on.

'Yes, he told me what he knew. But I don't think it was enough. He didn't know the answer to your questions, so if your threat is genuine, I suppose he will have to leave tonight.'

'Yes, madam, my threat was genuine. But exactly what did he tell you?'

She did not reply for a moment but went to the window and stared out at the dreary expanse of brick and concrete.

'What did he say? He said that when he was certain that the camp was going to fall into Allied hands he deserted. He went to Luneburg and stayed with a prostitute he knew.

'One day when he thought the search for him would have died down, he went out and met Steinberg in the street. He said she told him that she had escaped from the British, but gave no details at all. All she said was that her work was just beginning and he would hear of her again. She said that she had made a friend who would always stand by her. "A friend in science," was the expression she used.'

'I see, she said that, did she, "A friend in science". Did he tell you anything else?'

'About Steinberg, no, but he told me about himself. He told me he had lived with that Luneburg street walker till he had enough money to get a doctor to remove the S.S. tattoos from his arm. After that the paralysis started and she threw him out. That was when he sent for me.'

Kirk didn't look at her, but simply reached for the phone. 'That you, Inspector?' He spoke loudly so that the woman could hear. 'Yes, Kirk here. About that deportation order I gave you. Yes, that's right. Loser, to East Germany.

'Well, you can ignore it. No, no action is to be taken. Nothing is to be done about these people at all. Just forget the whole thing. Thank you.'

He looked up at the woman by the window.

For a moment she stared at him, her face working, and then without a word she turned and walked out of the room.

For a long time he sat very still beside his desk. Only his lips around the cigar moving.

Somewhere, in what she had told him, was the answer.

133

Somewhere in those words of Steinberg's was the key. He was sure of that. 'A friend. A friend in science.' He had all the facts now. All he needed, it was just a question of putting them together. She had told him where she was as certainly as if she had pointed to a place on the map. All he had to do was to arrange the pieces.

He pressed the buzzer before him and waited for his secretary.

'Well, Florrie, I think we've got it. It's all here now, all that remains is for you and I and Mrs. Mott to do a little hard work together. Now, ring down and ask them to send up some really black coffee. Then I want you to bring me all the files we have on this business. Everything. The Russian reports, Loser's, Roberts's, all you've got.

'After that, get through to the War Office. I want to know the full details of the repatriation of all allied female personnel during nineteen forty-six. In particular, I'd like to know if any of these women were unaccounted for after landing in the U.K. When you've done all that, tell old Mott I want her up here.'

*

It was after ten by the time the General finally pushed back his chair.

The atmosphere in the room was overpowering and the ashtray was piled high with cigar butts. Even the usually band-box Florrie looked weary and dishevelled.

'Well, ladies, I think that's it. We've got to be right, because there is no other possible alternative. It must have been that. Now, just two more errands, and then you can pack up and go home.

'I want the car outside in ten minutes. I'll take Queen and Willis with me and I want them armed. Yes, heavy automatic weapons, I think. I don't want to run into one of those creatures with just a revolver. When you've seen to that, get through to Hearn and that fellow Heath.'

He went to the cupboard and very carefully wrapped himself in his heaviest overcoat.

'You'd better speak to Heath first. Tell him I want him back in this office first thing in the morning. No, don't give him any details, something might go wrong even now. Just tell him to be here.'

'Very good, General, and Dr. Hearn?'

'Ah yes, Hearn.' He placed a muffler round his neck and drew on a pair of thick leather gloves.

134

'Give my compliments to the good Dr. Hearn and tell him to send somebody up to relieve Heath at once. Then you can say to him that if all goes well, I intend to introduce him to a very remarkable person in the morning.

'That, I think, is all. Good-night, ladies, and once more, thank you for your invaluable assistance.'

He bowed to them like an eighteenth-century beau and, swathed in warmth, moved out of the office, towards the car which was going to take him to Steinberg.

CHAPTER SIXTEEN

THERE was something dreadfully wrong with Roberts. Marcia saw it at once, even before she began to speak.

In the few hours since she had last seen him he had aged terribly. He was unshaven and haggard, and he seemed to have shrunk in his suit, like a pupa that had died in its cocoon.

His eyes were red rimmed and didn't seem able to focus properly. All the fire and resentment he had shown at the beginning of their last visit had left him.

'A question, but of course, Mrs. Heath, anything, anything at all. Do please come in.'

Once more she followed him into the dark, brown hall and once more the incense was like fog around them.

'I wonder if you'd mind coming upstairs to my little office, my dear,' he said. 'The drawing-room is in rather a state at the moment, I think we'd be more comfortable upstairs.'

She followed him up the long staircase, their feet sounding like drums on the bare lino, and she was struck by the size of the house. It had looked big enough from the street, but inside it was vast. The landing doubled back a long way, and then turned into a corridor.

They walked past door after door of empty rooms, and everywhere there was dust and debris, and peeling walls. It seemed impossible to believe that anybody could live there.

At last Roberts pushed open a door and motioned her to enter.

His office was as dreary as the rest of the house, but it was somehow efficient.

There was a steel filing cabinet in the corner and a modern

typewriter on the desk. The curtains were drawn, and it was lit by a single office lamp with a green shade.

He pulled a chair over for her and sat down himself.

'Now, my dear, what is it you wanted to know, how can I help you?'

'Professor Roberts,' she spoke quickly in her eagerness to prove or disprove her theory. 'Professor Roberts, you remember when Tony and I were last here, you described how you first saw Rosa Steinberg at the camp.'

'Yes, yes, of course I do, Mrs. Heath, after all, it's only two days ago, isn't it?' He smiled quietly at her.

'Yes, well you said that she was wearing battledress, didn't you?'

'Yes, that's right, I'm sure she was. It's a long time ago, but I'm certain that was what she was wearing.'

'Good. Now there is something else that I want to know. It's just an idea of mine. But if it's right I know how she escaped. Professor, just what kind of battledress was it?'

'What kind?' I don't understand. It was just an ordinary battledress, I think. They must have given it to her while they were searching her clothes. Why do you want to know this, Mrs. Heath? He ran his tongue over his grey lips.

Marcia thought for a moment and then made a quick decision.

'Professor Roberts,' she said. 'We've got to find Steinberg. We must find her, and we're almost sure she is alive. Now if you can tell me about that battledress and if it fits in with my idea, then I think I know what happened to her. Are you sure it was just an ordinary one? Do try and remember. Wasn't it a woman's and wasn't it blue, Professor?'

Roberts put his hands to his forehead and was silent for a moment.

'No, Mrs. Heath,' he said at last. 'It's no good, I just can't remember. I'd like to help you, but I just can't be sure. I think it was just an ordinary khaki battledress that one of the soldiers had lent her, but I'm not certain, it's long ago and I didn't pay a lot of attention to her clothes. I was only thinking about the work of the camp, you see.

'Just a minute, though. There is something that might help to refresh my memory. When you left the other morning, I tried to put down a few notes about Ruhleben. Anything at all that came to my mind. I was going to send them to your husband when I'd finished. I wonder if I went through them they might help me to remember that battledress.'

He rummaged among the drawers of his desk and then got up. 'No, they don't seem to be here. I must have left them

136

downstairs. Just wait here a moment and I'll go and get them.'

Left alone, Marcia sat stiffly in her chair. She was very, very disappointed. If only he could remember she would know. One way or the other she had to know. But she was almost sure he wouldn't be able to remember.

It was very dark in the room. The lamp threw a green beam over the desk and that was all. No light came from the curtained windows. A little clock ticked noisily on the mantelpiece, and far below in the street she could hear children singing.

Their voices were very faint behind the curtain. It was as if they were in another world. She could just make out the words:

'Here is a candle to light you to bed,
Here is a chopper to—'

The last line was cut off by the roar of a passing lorry.

She felt terribly alone in that room. If only Roberts would hurry up. Five minutes. What on earth was he doing. He must have found the notes by now.

She looked again at the madly ticking clock. Ten minutes. What could he be doing?

And suddenly she was frightened. She sat rigidly in the chair and was frightened, because she knew. She knew she was no longer alone in the room.

There was no movement, no motion, just behind her she could hear a soft breathing.

While she had been listening to the children, while the house had shaken with the passing lorry, someone had come into the room.

She gripped the arms of the chair and then forced herself to turn round.

Then she gasped with relief.

'Why, Mary,' she said, 'how your startled me.'

The idiot stood a little way back from the chair and she looked taller in the shadow of the lamp. She had a bundle over her left arm.

She smiled at Marcia and then did a very strange thing.

She took off her spectacles and put them on the chest by her side, and without them her eyes were no longer dull and vacant, but very bright, very intelligent eyes.

She lifted her free right hand again and suddenly her dark shining hair was just stuff on the floor, and her own hair showed, dull and lifeless.

She held out the bundle to Marcia and when she spoke, her voice was a dry, hard voice.

'Yes, you were quite right, Mrs. Heath, the battledress was blue,' said Rosa Steinberg.

CHAPTER SEVENTEEN

MISS SOPER stood on her civic rights.

She had been detained now for over a day and a half and she was very, very annoyed.

She blazed at Tony and Briggs and demanded to see a lawyer, a minister of religion, the lord lieutenant, her member of parliament.

Although she had been badly shaken by what she had seen in the cottage, time is a healer, and fear had long since turned to fury.

No, she did not for one moment believe that she had been detained for so long because of the epidemic. It was clearly a case of some vile conspiracy between the police, Dr. Jacques, Mr. Heath, and above all Colonel Briggs.

For what purpose she refused to say, but her grimly shut lips showed that she suspected the worst.

'But, my dear young lady, I assure you.' Briggs struggled to keep his voice controlled.

'You assure me, I don't need any assurance from you, thank you, Colonel. I know all about you. Mr. Shepherd spoke about people like you when you supported Sunday cinemas. Hundreds of black women, people like you kept in India, he said. You—you Mammon of unrighteousness.'

For a second Tony feared that Briggs was about to have a stroke. His normally dark face went a dull, sooty black. He clutched his throat, and when he spoke, he formed his words with difficulty.

'Come on, Heath—no point in continuing this—this conversation—no point at all. And, young woman, you will stay here till you're told to go.' He turned smartly on his heel and marched out of the door.

'Phew, what a tartar. Glad to be out of that. See her point though. No fun being shut in there all that time. No fun at all. Still, Black Women, Mammon of Unrighteousness.' He blew his nose violently with a large purple handkerchief.

'Must have something to go on before long though—very difficult position—very difficult indeed. Must have more definite orders—nothing at the moment except old Kirk's instructions.

'Government'll have to speak soon, you know. Can't keep this place shut off indefinitely—got the Lord Lieutenant on my neck already, and I expect that that chap Wilkinson—wretched radical feller, will be after me soon. Must have something.'

'You're quite right, Colonel. But I spoke on the phone to Kirk an hour ago. He's doing all he can to get the P.M. to make a public announcement. The trouble is that they're terrified of disturbances. Still, he thinks they will tomorrow, at the latest.'

'Good, glad to hear it. Very glad. About time, too. Well, what is it, Rogers?'

The uniformed constable saluted and spoke to Briggs as if he was addressing a large and dangerous dog.

'Beg pardon, sir, but the Super says will you come at once, sir. It's them reporters, sir. We can't get rid of 'em. Keep saying they're going to stay till they've seen you. And Mr. Wilkinson, the member of parliament, is there as well, sir. Say they'll stay all night, if need be. Very embarrassing for the Super, sir.'

'Damn you, Rogers, and damn your Superintendent too.' Briggs quivered in his rage. 'Good God, constable! You chaps seem to want a nursemaid to run after you. About thirty great strapping hulking fellers sitting about all day, drinking tea and playing billiards, and when it comes to a push, you can't even get rid of a few reporters. Very well then, if I must go, I must. You'll come with me, won't you, Heath? Try and give these chaps a bit of technical jargon. Only way to quieten 'em.'

He led the way to the police car as to a firing squad.

'Oh, Mr. Heath.' It was a nurse who interrupted them this time. The same sister whom he had first seen when he had come to the hospital.

'You're wanted on the telephone, Mr. Heath. It was a woman, the secretary of a General Kirk. She said it was most important you spoke to her.'

Oh, thank you, Sister. Would you excuse me a moment, Colonel Briggs. I'll be as quick as I can.'

'Take your time, old boy, take your time. God knows I'm in no hurry to meet these, these gentlemen.'

Tony went into the Matron's office and took up the phone. 'Hullo, Heath speaking.'

'Oh, Mr. Heath, I'm so glad I caught you. Yes, this is Miss Bond, General Kirk's secretary.

'No, the General is not here at the moment, but he asked

me to tell you to get back to London first thing tomorrow morning.'

'Tomorrow morning! But that's quite impossible, Miss Bond. I can't possibly leave here. Besides it's just ten now.'

'I'm very sorry, Mr. Heath, but the General's orders were quite definite. It is most important that you come to this office. Yes, they are sending somebody from Farhill to take your place.'

'Very well, Miss Bond. I suppose I'll have to come. Didn't General Kirk give you any reason for this change of plan?'

'No, I'm sorry, Mr. Heath, but the General doesn't take me into his confidence. What time shall we expect you?'

'Let me see. I've got one or two things I must check up here before I leave, and the helicopter has gone. I should say I could get to your office by about eight.'

'Thank you, Mr. Heath, till eight o'clock then. Good-bye.'
There was a click and the line went dead.

Tony walked back to Briggs like a man in a dream. He couldn't for one moment understand this change of plan.

What on earth was Kirk up to? Here was the storm centre, here was where the next attack would come, here was the heart of the matter.

What could this sudden recall mean? It seemed crazy. And yet after all Kirk was in charge, and he trusted Kirk completely.

He leaned through the window of the police car and explained the position to Briggs.

'Umph, I see, so you're going. That means I'll have to face these fellers alone. No, no, my boy, you get off at once. No point in hanging about here, I'll take care of everything. If you go soon, you'll have time for a wash and a bite to eat before you get to Kirk.

'Now, you'll want a car, won't you? What kind, eh? Do you want one of these fellers driving you? Or would you rather be on your own?' He looked at the stolid back before him. 'Yes, quite so. Prefer it that way myself. Sure though? You could sleep behind one of these chaps, you know.

'Well, what you'd better do is to take my Betty. If you can drive at all, she'll get you there quick enough. You'll find her just behind the hospital, and she's full of juice. Go carefully though, boy. I shouldn't say it, but I like her better than most people I know.

'Well, you say your relief will be here soon. Good luck, boy, and all the best.'

He gave the key to Tony, held out a lean, hard hand and was driven off to the waiting reporters like a sheep to the slaughter.

The Colonel's Bentley was as old and cantankerous as her master, but she came from a good family and went like the wind. Tony sat in her high seat and revelled in the deep, slow throb of the long stroke engine, the feel of her enormous steering wheel, and the wind that swept over her pretence of a screen. She was so strong, so healthy, so very much the lady. He felt joy in her, and joy in the fresh sea, salt air that rushed around him.

With her long, smooth motion, his tiredness was swept away. And yet, he was still tired. He had had only a few hours' sleep during the last four days. He was very tired.

He looked at his watch. With Betty, he could be in London hours before eight.

He would treat himself to one small indulgence.

He slowed down before a big, pretentious pub and pulled the Bentley into the car park.

He ignored the disapproving stare of the young lady behind the bar, as she noticed his unshaven chin and rumpled clothes, and ordered a double whisky. Then he asked for the phone.

It took him a long time to get through. First he had to get the number from the exchange, and when he did, all the lines to Wales were suddenly engaged at once.

He could hear them calling for last orders in the bars as the ringing tone finally reached him.

'Oh, is that you, Joan,' he said. 'Yes, Tony Heath here. I wonder if I could speak to Marcia for a moment.'

'Oh, Tony.' She seemed terribly relieved at the end of the line. 'Tony, I'm so glad you rang. We've been getting a bit worried about Marcia. She hasn't reached us yet.'

'What's that? You mean she's not with you?'

'No, Tony, she rang us latish last night and said she would be coming down in time for lunch. Then this morning we had a telegram from her saying she was coming later. About seven, she said. Hang on a moment, Tony, I think I've got it here.

'Yes, that's it. This is what it says:

' "Coming via Durford to collect things, hope to be with you seven." '

'I see, Joan.' His voice was very strained. 'Tell me, is there a later train she could have got if she'd missed the connexion?'

'No, sorry, Tony, we checked that. There was one that got in a few minutes ago. We went down and met it. There was no sign of her. But don't worry, Tony, I'm sure everything is all right. She most probably missed the connexion at Durford, and decided to stay the night there. We would have phoned

141

her, but we couldn't get the number. I'm sure everything is all right.'

'Yes. Yes, Joan, I'm sure you're right. Thank you very much for trying. You wouldn't have got the number, we've only had the phone a day or two. Yes, I'm certain that's what she's done. She might have rung you though. Yes, I'll let you know when she's coming. Thanks so much, Joan. Goodnight.'

Before he put down the receiver, he knew that something was wrong. Marcia might have gone to Durford to collect her things. She might have missed the connexion and decided to stay the night at home. But it was still wrong. Whatever had happened she would have phoned them. She would have let them know what she was doing, that she would be late.

It was with no hope at all that he dialled the Durford number ; and he was right. After five minutes, he put down the phone. Nobody was there.

They were already emptying the bar as he went back for his drink. He saw the girl behind the counter look coldly at him as he took up his glass and drained the whisky at a gulp, his hand shaking and a few drops spilling on his coat.

'Excuse me, sir, excuse me one moment.'

He turned and saw a large, dark-suited man standing in front of him. 'Excuse me, but I'm the manager here. Have you by any chance got a car outside, sir?'

Tony nodded.

'I see, sir, sure you're feeling all right, sir, quite up to driving?'

For a moment, Tony felt like cursing the man, hitting him for his impertinence. Driving his fist into the dark fleshy face. Kicking him as he fell.

Then his judgement came into play. Whatever happened he had to control himself. Keep calm, take the insult. There must be no delay.

'Yes, thank you, I'm quite all right, quite all right.' He put down his glass and strode past him, out into the yard where Betty waited like an aged queen among the shiny minnows of the car park.

'What was she doing, why didn't she ring, where had she gone?' He kept asking himself as the enormous headlights cut through the night and the heavy engine hurled him south.

Why? It was so out of character. She had promised to go to Wales. She had told her friends she was going. What had happened to her? She was punctilious about keeping appointments and promises. Something had to be wrong.

He had to hurry to London. Kirk would never have recalled him if it wasn't vital, but all the same he must know.

142

He pulled the Bentley into the side of the road and fumbled in the dashboard cupboard. As he had thought, Briggs carried a dog-eared map. He flicked through its stained pages, and yes, it was easy. He wouldn't lose any time at all.

Another twenty miles, and there was a turning to the right that would take him to Durford in a few minutes. He could go there, see if Marcia had been, and still get to Kirk in good time. He pushed the map back into the pocket, let in the clutch, and with his exhaust blaring like gun fire swept down the empty road.

The cathedral clock was striking midnight as he turned into the quad. Immensely lost and far away, the gigantic notes sounded sadly over the sleeping town.

An early sleeping town. Everything was out now. Everyone was in bed. Everything shut and put away. A few faint strings of lights up the hill. A dull glow in a corner of the docks, but all house lamps cold, and the curtains drawn. His own windows were like blind eyes in the moonlight.

As soon as he opened the door he knew that she had been there. Her case lay by the door and her coat was thrown over the chair. There was a faint reminder of perfume.

But more than that, more than the case, the coat, the lingering scent, there was the indefinable atmosphere that he knew so well. She had been there.

He called her name and then went upstairs. He put on the landing light as he went up, calling again softly, so as not to startle her, and opened the bedroom door.

It was no good. She was not there. The bed lay crisp and made up and the room was in apple-pie order.

He crossed to the wicker clothes basket and opened the lid. And yes, she had been there. She had changed her things and then gone out of the house, leaving her coat and case in the living-room.

He walked slowly down the stairs, and at each tread fear was walking softly behind him.

Yes, she had been home. She had thrown her coat over the chair and gone upstairs and changed. She had come down and sat on the sofa for a moment. The cushion was the only rumpled thing in the room, and beside the sofa, on the little table, was a half-empty cup.

She had sat on the sofa, drinking her coffee and then suddenly she had got up and gone out. Gone out on the spur of the moment without even time to take her things, to phone her friends.

Why, how long ago, for what reason? What could have made her do it? What could have made her act so strangely?

143

He opened the desk and pulled out a time table. She was to have been with Joan at seven, there must be a train that tied up with that time.

Yes, here it was, she would have had to have left Durford at two-thirty. Two-thirty, it was now after twelve. Nine and a half hours had passed.

He threw the book on to the desk, turned round and looked at the crumpled chair, the sofa, the half drunk cup of coffee, and then suddenly noticed the scrap of paper beside it.

At first it meant nothing at all to him. The sketchy notes and sentences seemed completely without meaning. Then he remembered Marcia's habit of always putting things on paper before she came to a decision, and the words began to take form.

He stared hard at them. Somewhere in those scrawled notes was the answer to where she had gone. He must work it out.

'If b'drss not soldier's. Impossible escape then. Coffin daughter says women there. If right, Steinberg still with Loser. R. Must remember. Ask R.'

'Ask R.' There was only one person in the affair who could be R. She had gone to see Roberts then, to ask him something that he hadn't remembered. Something to do with a battledress.

A battledress. But no, that wasn't important, it was Roberts who was important. Roberts who hadn't remembered something. Roberts to whom Marcia had gone over nine and a half hours ago. Tony leaned for a moment against the wall, and his eyes were no longer quite sane. Roberts might have forgotten, but *he* was remembering. Remembering his last talk with Hearn. Remembering telling him something that both of them considered obvious and unimportant. Remembering the smell of a hospital ward ; and as he remembered he knew. Everything fitted exactly into place, and he knew. Knew why Roberts's house was filled with incense.

He turned and rushed across the room and through the hall to the front door and the final meeting.

*

The plain clothes driver looked what he was, a respectable family man, but he drove like a maniac. The tyres screamed in agony on the gravel of the corners and the headlights swung in and out of the long streams of lorries and trailers like scythes, as the car fled to the North.

In the back, the two men whom Kirk had taken with him

144

sat very respectfully listening to their chief who lounged in the corner, shrouded in rugs.

They were very ordinary looking men, small and nondescript, and they would never have been noticed in a crowd, which was one of the reasons why they held their jobs. Only their eyes gave them away. Very shrewd, very cold eyes and they rarely smiled with them.

Kirk paused for a moment in his talk as the car slowed slightly in a narrow village street, and picking up the speaking tube, bawled at the driver.

'What the hell do you think you're playing at, Hodgetts. I said I wanted to get there quickly, didn't I, and here you are dawdling about as if you had all the time in the world, and three nervous dowagers behind you. Get your foot down on that ruddy accelerator, man, and keep it there.' He snapped the instrument back into its cupboard and turned once more to his colleagues.

'Well, boys, I think that is all you need to know, for the present anyhow. But there is no margin for even the slightest mistake. I don't for one moment think that we'll be expected, but we're not going to take any chances. That's why you're so heavily armed. If one of those things so much as shows itself I want you to tear it right apart.

'With the man and the woman it's different. If there is the slightest possibility of escape, shoot. But only to cripple. I can't afford any chancy death-bed confessions. So get that quite clear. Shoot if you have to, but only to cripple. I want them both in good state. Remember that, and remember as well that if anything goes wrong, I'll break you. Break you both. Well, that's that. Now you can relax, boys.'

He looked at his watch. 'Yes, there's plenty of time, unfortunately. With that old woman Hodgetts in front of us, it'll be another two hours before we get there. Plenty of time for a game, eh?'

He reached into his pocket and drew out a small ivory chess set.

'Well, which of you is it to be? I think you, Peter, this time. Come on to this bucket seat in front of me. We should be able to see all right. That's better. I'll give you a castle, and remember if you beat me you can start asking for promotion when we get home.'

The car tore on over the flat lands of the Midlands. Its tyres slipped and screamed on the gravel and the engine howled in agony as the stolid man in front carried out his master's orders. In the dashboard in front of him the two enemies, time

145

and speed, glowed in their cases, one needle contending with another as they raced to Durford.

In the back all was quiet. Kirk's cigar glowed over the board, and from time to time he lifted his twisted hand and moved a piece. Very soon the game was over. He thanked his opponent, complimented him on his improved play, and then put away the board and leaned back.

He looked out for a while at the dark, spinning countryside and then over to the hard eyes of his companions. Whatever happened he could rely on them implicitly.

As long as they didn't suspect, as long as they didn't know that he was coming, it would be all right. He had almost finished the game now. His opponent's fallen pieces were all stacked neatly before him. He knew exactly what moves he had still to make, how many squares were still filled.

All he had to do was to lift a piece, move it across the board and say 'Mate'.

There was only one problem left in the game. When he did move, would he have managed to move in time?

*

It was raining hard when Tony came out into the quad and the moon was far behind the black billowing clouds.

He ran stumbling through the rain to the Bentley, pulled himself in, and pushed the starter, felt the huge engine pulse into life. He knew quite well what he should do. What he had to do, but there was no time.

He should have waited, gone to the police, had the house surrounded, but he couldn't afford the time. There was no time. Why even now—

He pushed the thought out of his mind and hurled the big car madly across the square and down the steep hill, its wheels slipping and skidding on the wet cobbles.

He parked a little way from the house, whatever happened they mustn't know he was coming, and fumbled in the tool chest. He was right, Briggs was a careful motorist. He brought out a heavy electric torch and a rusty tyre lever with a sharpened end. With them he could manage.

He walked quietly down the street, cursing the slight sound of his feet on the streaming pavement, confident in the feel of the lever in his hand. Very far away a ship's siren echoed from the mouth of the river, and somewhere near at hand a rat screamed in agony.

He was there now. The house in front of him, tall as a mountain in the dim light, its windows like black empty caves.

Very carefully he pushed open the rusty gate and walked on his toes across the garden.

It was easy, much easier than he thought. His lever sank between door and post. With hardly a sound, the rotten wood gave and the door swung a little way open.

Once again he took the sharp lever and pushed it between two links of the chain. He gave a sudden, quick twist, and with a slight whisper of tearing metal, stepped through into the dim hall.

There was not a sound anywhere. He swung his torch round, looking for a lead, looking at the dull brown pictures, the peeling paint, the chipped doors, a way to go.

He moved towards the foot of the staircase and then paused as a floorboard creaked beneath his feet. He must be careful, whatever happened they must not know he was there till he had found her.

He waited for a moment and then stiffened. The board moved again. Although he was motionless it still moved. It was not his feet that were moving the boards. Someone was beside him. He swung wildly round towards the moving boards, bringing his torch round to them and almost reached them when the blow fell. It fell on the side of his head, flat and dull and heavy. He gasped under it, tried to fight it, and then the light came on.

It came suddenly, straight between his eyes like a flame and it was terribly beautiful. It was white and blue and gold, and all the colours of the rainbow. It was so beautiful that it took away the pain in his head.

He tried to ignore it for a moment, to turn from it and hurl himself on to the figure at his side, but it was no good. The light was too strong, too bright, too wonderful. The very meaning of life was just at the end of that unwavering beam. He had to follow the light, to sink into it, to become part of the light.

He sank slowly to his knees and lay still on the dusty floor of the hall.

CHAPTER EIGHTEEN

HE was lying in the sun, and the sun was very painful in his eyes. He was lying on the white wall of a mountain in the sun, and he had to get up. He had to get up and walk on to the summit, but not just now. Just now he had to lie very still and wait for the pain to die.

'Even so,' said a voice beyond him, and it was a tight hard voice like an overstretched wire. 'Even so, he's coming round,' and the voice was just beyond the pain in his head.

He forced himself to open his eyes and look at the voice, and in front of him was Marcia.

She sat before him on a chair and she didn't move at all. She smiled at him as he opened his eyes and seemed to strain forward, but she didn't move.

'Why doesn't she come to me?' he thought. 'Why doesn't she get up and come over to me? Ah well, if she won't, I must go to her.'

He struggled to get up to his feet and walk over to her, but it was no good. His arms were tight behind his back and something held his hands. 'Stay still,' said the voice, 'just stay very still. You can't move at all, Mr. Heath, so just stay exactly as you are.'

He looked past Marcia, past the table, past the huge white cabinet with the glass instruments, and behind them all was the voice.

Rosa Steinberg leaned against the wall of the laboratory and he knew her.

He knew her and what she was at once. Knew her without her false hair, her spectacles, her vacant hanging expression. Knew her by her cold, intelligent face, her lank hair, and the bright piercing eyes. The eyes with something wrong with them. The eyes of the unloved and the unloving, and the other thing behind the eyes.

'So, so it was you, Mary,' he said slowly and his mouth was thick and full of salt. 'All the time, right under our noses, it was you.'

Steinberg laughed. There was nothing of mirth or humour in her action, it had nothing to do with the conventional idea of laughter, it was merely a sound.

148

'Yes, it was I. All the time I was here waiting for you, and you never knew, never guessed, never suspected, until this little fool thought she would play detective and led you here, right into the hollow of my hand.'

She swung her hard eyes at Marcia, and as she turned, Tony seemed to look through her eyes at the lost years behind them. The years of the cellars, the hunger, the burning city, and the things that had walked it. And suddenly he knew what he was dealing with, for in her terrible way, the woman was a patriot.

'Why do you think I showed you who I was, my dear?' she said, and her voice was very low and gentle. 'Why didn't I just go on with the game and let Roberts tell you that the uniform was khaki? You'd have gone away, then, quite satisfied and forgotten your little theory, wouldn't you? Well, I showed myself because I need your help. I need you to persuade your husband to answer three easy questions. Firstly, Mr. Heath, I want to know just why the establishment at Farhill and the British Government have begun to take such an interest in me ; secondly, how much do they know and how far are they behind me,' and once more she smiled her terrible smile at him, 'and lastly I want you to tell me all the latest news from Russia.

'Oh yes, Mr. Heath. I'm quite certain that you have no intention of telling me anything at all. No British gentleman ever gives in to threats, does he? And don't worry, nobody is going to do anything to either of you. Nobody is going to put a cigarette to your wife's nice neck or twist her arm. Nothing is going to be done at all. All I'm going to do is to leave you alone for a time.' She walked across the room, and then paused at the door. 'While I'm away, you might do one thing for me, though. I'd like you to look at that wall.'

Tony looked in front of him and suddenly stiffened. The wall itself was just the same as the others. It was painted a bright shiny green and was bare of ornament. There was only one thing about it that was remarkable. There was a brass handle in the centre of it, and around the handle, a thin hairline crack which could only be the outline of an air-tight door. He knew with utter certainty what would be behind that door.

'Yes, you see it, don't you, Mr. Heath? You see the handle. Well, it can be opened from here, but there is also another lever in the next room. What I propose to do is this. I shall go into that room and leave you alone for ten minutes. If, before those ten minutes are up, you decide to answer my questions, you have only to press the bell by your hands. Yes, you can reach it. When I hear the bell, I will come back and you will tell me what I want to know.

'If, however, the bell does not ring in ten minutes, then I will pull the lever and that door will open.

'You see, I have you both ways, Mr. Heath. If you talk, well and good, if not, then you cannot have the slightest inkling of what that door hides and you are of no use to me.'

She moved quietly to the door, half opened it and then looked very hard at Tony. 'Do something when you are alone, Mr. Heath. You are a biologist, so think about your trade. Ponder a little on the power of the smaller plants about the world.' She smiled at him and was gone.

'The power of the smaller plants about the world.' Before she had finished speaking, Tony's head was clear and the pain left him. 'The power of the plant.' Suddenly, for the first time, he understood fully what they were up against. Knew completely. He had seen two cases of the thing, one dead, the other half developed. They had told him a little of its structure and development. Now there was something else. He had thought of it as a tragedy, a disease, a case history. The fear had been for its spread, not for itself. For it, he had only felt an immense pity and compassion ; but suddenly it was real and personal to him, because he knew. 'The power of the plant.' The thin strands of mistletoe killing an oak, the concrete cracking over the soft grass, the white fingers of lacrymans in the joist. Now he knew the violence that would go with its propagation. Knew what the Russians had fought so clumsily and so long. Knew just how the *Gadshill*'s sailors had died. Knew that what they were facing was not just a freak, a monster, a thing of pity, but a species on the march. A race, with a terrible hatred in its will to survive. Knew that a second after the steel door swung open they would be torn to pieces.

'Marcia, Marcia, my darling, are you all right, have they done anything to you?' He struggled to keep his voice calm.

'Yes, yes, Tony, I'm all right, but the door, Tony!' Her words were shrill with hysteria. 'Tony, you must tell her what she wants. You must tell her. She's mad, Tony. She'll open the door and I know what's behind it. Oh God, Tony, you must. Please ring the bell.'

He looked at her face, looked at her arms straining at the cords that held her and the hairline crack in the wall behind her. He forced himself to speak firmly.

'Darling, keep calm. We must hold her off, we must delay her if we can, so try and keep calm. Hold on to yourself and everything will be all right.' He hated what he said, hated the

150

thought of what he was exposing her to, but he had to play the game to the end, to the final throw.

'Now listen, listen, my darling. My hands are tied to the pipe behind me and I can't move at all, but if you could jerk your chair across the room to me, you might get me free. Come on, darling, try it.'

With a sudden effort of will, she seemed to pull herself together and nodded. She jerked against the cords, and with the movement, the chair slid forwards a little. The clock on the table showed seven minutes to go.

She made slow progress, her feet were firmly strapped to the chair legs and off the ground, but all the same she came to him. Inch by inch the chair creaked across the floor towards him, and at each movement, the hand of the clock seemed to slide forward a little too. There were four minutes left when she was beside him.

'Good, well done, darling, well done, my clever darling. Just a little more. That's right. Now try and turn round a little. Back a bit. Good. Now can you get your fingers on to the knots? I'll let my wrists go slack. Try and see if you can undo them.'

There were two minutes to go. She leaned backwards against him, and her fingers tore at the cords with every atom of strength in them. 'Tony, can you twist your arm round a bit? I can't get past it. Yes, that's better. I think I've almost got it now. Just a little more and—yes, it's coming—Tony!' Her voice suddenly rose to a scream. 'Oh, Tony, the clock, look at the clock.'

And suddenly there was no more time. The pointer stood on the mark, the ten minutes were over. From the wall came a dull, metallic click. Tony gave one final wrench at his bonds, felt them part slightly, felt them slip a little way up his wrists, slip again and hold.

He stared at the clock, stared at the hair's breadth crack which was slowly widening, and pressed the bell.

She came into the room like a shadow and once more took up her position by the table.

'You were just in time,' she said, 'just in time. Another five seconds and it would have been too late. The door would have opened, and then nothing on this earth could have saved you. Well, you have decided. Now, my questions, please, Mr. Heath.'

Tony was silent for a moment. Whatever happened, he had to play for time. It didn't matter very much what he told Steinberg, what mattered was how long he could keep her there. He could feel his wrists looser now. If he could only

151

work them a little more he would be free. Besides there was Kirk. Kirk had said that he would bring her in, that something was going to happen in the morning. Kirk might be wrong, of course, but he didn't think so. In any case he had to hold her, make her talk, provoke her if necessary to make her talk, but keep her where she was.

'Your questions. Very well, I shall answer them. I shall answer them in one sentence. You are finished.'

He looked at her and watched her lips slowly draw up over her teeth like a wolf's.

'Yes, Fräulein Steinberg, you are finished. We know about you, we know what you have done, and we have beaten it. Three days ago the counter radiations were perfected and your monsters will soon be without meaning. You have killed a few people in Russia, but that is all. In a day or two, the authorities will find out who you are, and that will be the end of you. And it will be a dreadful end, Fräulein. They won't even allow you to die, you know. They won't even punish you. They will merely pity you and shut you away. In a few years you will only be a tale to frighten children.'

It was working. The skin was tight over her skull and her face was no longer human. When she spoke, her words were slurred and indistinct.

'You lie, you lie, Heath. Nobody can stop them now. You have had no time to stop them. It would have taken you months to find the radiations and you've had no months, only days. There are only two places, where the radiation figures are stored, in my head, and here.' She put her hand on a small case on the table before her. 'No, you're lying. There is nothing that can stop the seeds I made. Nothing. Nobody knows how to stop them.'

'Roberts knows.' It was Marcia who spoke. 'Roberts knows, and perhaps Roberts has talked.'

'Roberts! Roberts knows nothing, nothing at all. Roberts was merely a tool that I used. A means to an end. You would get nothing from Roberts.'

'A tool, Fräulein,' Tony broke in. 'A means to your end. The end being complete and utter destruction of everything you hate, isn't it? Well, I can understand that. I know you. I can imagine why you did the things that you have done. I can see the motives in your face and your past. I know what you have become. A quite impersonal force of evil let loose in the world. I know what you follow. The creatures you made are the children of that thing working through you. All that I can understand. But not Roberts. I can't understand Roberts. Tell me, how did you do it? How did you get a man like Roberts,

152

a supposedly reasonable man, an intelligent man, the holder of a chair in a university. How did you get him to condone, or help you in your aim?'

Once again she laughed, and the laugh was not only for him or Marcia, but for Roberts. For Roberts and Tony and Marcia and all the world and the mindless things that walked the Russian plains. And as she laughed, he knew that it was working. She would talk now. She had to talk. They were her first audience and she would tell them about everything. She would talk for hours, and if only Kirk was right, there was still a chance left for them.

'My aim, what do you know of my aim or what I am? Nothing! We will win, Mr. Heath, and there is nothing you can ever do to stop us. Sometimes you think you have won, but you are always wrong, because on us the sun will never set. Yes, never set, Mr. Heath. Don't you remember our marching song, *"Für uns wird die Sonne niemals untergeben".'*
Her voice was suddenly soft and low again.

'But Roberts, my dear. Yes, I will tell you about Roberts.' She smiled at them, and settled herself more comfortably against the table.

'There was once a man, Mrs. Heath, who was all wrong inside. I don't mean wrong in the religious or medical sense. I don't mean he had a devil or a neurosis. I mean he was wrong for what he had to do. When that man was a little boy he used to play with a chemistry set. He played with it all day, to the exclusion of all other interests, and because of that play his doting parents thought he was to become a scientific genius. In time, he began to think so too.

'He went to the University and did quite well. He got decent degrees and at last he came to this place as an assistant lecturer. Very nice, wasn't it, the young Chopin, the boy genius was starting in the world. There was only one thing wrong in the picture. He wasn't a genius, he was only a competent technician, and soon he wasn't even young. That could have been all right, of course. A lot of people think they are what they're not, but in time they realize their limitations and accept themselves.

'But not him. You see, he made no friends. Not a single friend. No one to tell him the truth. No yardstick to measure his ability.

'He spent all his spare time in his room, conducting experiments which never worked. Producing formulae which were valueless, always believing that one day it would come off, that one fine morning the world would wake up and know what he was.

153

'There was only one person who knew about this. One girl student. A rather stupid girl, I imagine. He talked to her, told her of his great promise, and she believed him.

'She believed in him enough to marry him. They married and took this house here, so they could be completely on their own. They moved in and she worshipped him. Worshipped him as a god, until a week was over, and she knew her god was sexually incapable.

'I think that woman must have prayed for the death which she found five years later.

'After that he knew himself for what he was. He knew it, but he wouldn't accept it. Although he himself had no talent, he believed there was a power outside of himself, which would one day act through him. A power which would use him as its instrument. Soon he thought he would find that power.

'Well, he found it. He found it at exactly eleven o'clock on the fine bright morning of March the tenth, nineteen forty-five.'

She stopped and fumbled in a drawer and took out a cigarette. When she went on it seemed as if her words had nothing to do with her body, but as if something was speaking through her.

'He wasn't very happy in the Army. He was much older than his colleagues and he made no friends. Also there was not enough time for his dreams. He was almost at the end of his tether, when they sent him off to see what was happening at Ruhelben camp. And at Ruhelben he met it. He met the power that was going to put him on the map. He met me.

'I knew Roberts as soon as he came into the room. I knew what he wanted, what he dreamed about, what he hoped for, as clearly as if it was written on his face. Once I knew that, it was easy to make my offer.

'Roberts would help me escape. He would get me a place to hide in. A place where I could be completely undisturbed. And in return he would become one of the greatest biologists in the world.

'I think you know how it was managed, don't you? The girl's uniform, hiding in Bremen till I could get the papers forged, then the boat to Harwich, no questions asked, and the kind professor gives a home to his orphaned niece.

'I think that should answer your questions, Mr. Heath.'

'No, not quite, there is one more thing.' He must keep her talking, keep playing for time as long as possible, he was nearly free now.

'Just one more thing. Roberts was ready and willing to help you at the beginning, but did he know? Did he know what you were, what you were doing?'

'What I was. That's difficult to say. I don't even know that myself. He knew I was experimenting with mutants. He understood enough to see that. But he didn't realize the form. Nor did he know that I had only one aim in escaping from the British, in going on living. To finish my work.

'He argued about it at first, but having committed one crime, it was easy to drive him to more. He soon went to work for me. Those poor women who disappeared round here, Mrs. Heath, so terrible.' Her voice fell into the whine of the imbecile.

'Yes, he helped me. He got me the human subjects, and the Madura which was rather more difficult, but he got it. The one thing the good professor doesn't know is that I have used what I made.

'His idea was very muddled. He wanted to do good through evil. We were to provide a deterrent to war. To give the world a threat which would make the atom bomb look like a picnic. Which would ensure peace. He still thinks that. He has never begun to realize that unlike the Hebrew prophet "I have not come to fulfil but to destroy".'

She put back her head and laughed and all at once it was not she who was laughing, but something within her. It was something else's laughter, and huge lips and lungs were behind it.

It rang and echoed like thunder around the bare walls of the laboratory and rattled on the steel furniture and the glass, and then suddenly stopped as if it were gagged.

'You—let—them—loose.'

Roberts stood in the doorway, and for the first time his grey face was alive. His voice was thick and muddy and very deliberate and sounded like something rotten being pulled apart.

'You—let—them—loose. After all your promises, you let them loose and spread the spores.'

He turned to Tony, waving his hands wildly in front of him.

'Yes, I did it, Heath. I helped her. I committed murder for her. Those women who disappeared, it was I. But I, we, I never intended this. You have to believe me, Heath. I never intended she should do this. I was insane. I probably still am, but not this, I never wanted this.'

He covered his face with his hands and then straightened, and his face was firm. 'We've got to stop it, you know. We've got to. If it spreads—Still, there's time. If you have the counter radiations it can be checked. We've got to stop it. Got to. I'll let you free.'

He moved towards Tony and paused as Steinberg spoke.

155

'Just stay still, Roberts. Stay very still or I'll kill you.' She had turned to the desk and opened a drawer to take something out. The black automatic looked too heavy for her tiny hand.

'Just stay still and do nothing. There is nothing you can do. It is finished. The spores are free, the only record of the radiations is with me, the business is over. So just stay very still.'

Roberts looked up at her and then began to walk forwards, talking as he went.

'Rosa, my dear, give me the gun. You're sick, Rosa. We both are, but now we've got to come out of the dream and wake up. We've got to, Rosa, we've got to stop it, so give me the gun, my dear.' He was like a father speaking to his child. 'Give it to me, Rosa.'

He was almost up to her. His thin worn hand was writhing like a snake in front of him to the barrel of the automatic, when she fired. She fired four shots, the heavy Luger jumping in her hand as it exploded in front of him, and his arm went down. His arm went down to his side and an expression of complete bewilderment came on to his face. His legs bent under him, till he was crouching on the floor, and very slowly his hand seemed to creep forwards to her feet. Then he died.

Tony and Marcia sat stiffly in their chairs, and although they were shocked and horrified by Roberts's death, they were no longer afraid. They were no longer afraid because they had heard.

Above the roar of the gun and the falling body they had heard the noise below. The crash of the door and the feet in the hall.

And Steinberg heard it too. They saw her stiffen like an animal and slowly bring the gun up again till it was pointed at Marcia. It shook slightly as her finger whitened on the trigger, and then suddenly she changed her mind. She turned and reached at something behind her, seized the case, and dashed for the door.

Tony made his last effort. Whatever happened he had to stop her now. Let her get away for a minute, let her be free long enough to destroy her papers and they were finished.

He tore at his wrists, felt the cords hold for a second and break, then hurled himself to the door.

They reached it together. Her fingers with the case clawing at him and the gun coming up. He heard the crash of the explosion, felt the red hot thing in his shoulder and then he had her.

He had her tight in his good arm and the gun was falling away from him. He gave a sudden heave and sent her spinning

156

back into the room. He stood dazed for a moment looking at the floor, when Marcia screamed.

He swung round and looked at her. She was sitting rigid in her chair, her eyes fixed across the room, screaming as if she was insane. And he didn't need to know why. Before he had even glanced beyond her to the wall she was looking at, he knew why.

While he was grappling with Steinberg, the door had been opening. It had opened smoothly, silently, efficiently, on well oiled hinges, and now something was coming out. Something monstrous was coming out. Something huge, much, much bigger than anything he had either seen or imagined. Something utterly horrible. The last form. The final complete mutation.

And Steinberg saw it too. She shrieked and scrabbled like a crab on the floor away from it. She mouthed words, and they were few and they didn't mean anything. 'Lee,' she said, 'Lee—Lee—Lee.' Over and over again she said it, and then 'Many'.

And then it was over. She didn't just die. There was no time for dying. Her end had nothing to do with the conventional idea of death. She was just there one moment and then not there. There was simply nothing of her there. Nothing left of her. Nothing that could even be called a part of her there. There was just stuff on the floor and the walls, and that was all there was.

Tony took up the chair in his one good hand and stood in front of his wife. He had no hope left of saving her, but he could still die for her. He held the chair in front of him, and it was like a toy before the thing that was coming.

The thing that was out of its tomb and was coming to him now.

Coming across the room, vast, monstrous, deadly, but still incredibly sad. Its smell was all around it as it came, the fresh, sad, haunting smell of hay, as it came over him. Came over with its no face above him and its no eyes looking at him and its no arms reaching for him. He lashed at it with the chair and waited for the end.

And then it happened. There was a great shouting and a noise like thunder behind him. He saw the thing stop and sway away from him. Sway away and then straighten and move forward again towards him. Move forward and brush the chair to matchwood in his hand. Reach for him, grasp him, and then reel backwards in flames, a mere mass of shapeless, blazing tissue as Kirk's explosive bullets tore it to pieces.

CHAPTER NINETEEN

THE police had nearly all left, the crowds had gone home, a little grey was creeping through the dusty window when at last Tony pushed the papers across to Kirk.

He sat with Marcia beside him at Roberts's dining-room table, and although he was very pale and his arm was bound he could smile at last.

'Well, General, that's it,' he said. 'We've got it all now, the lot. Why, she even gives us the counter radiations in full. It's up to Hearn now. Get these papers to him as soon as you can, let him do a little routine laboratory work, and we've finished.'

'So we've made it after all, little lady,' said Kirk slowly, and for a moment his torn hand rested lightly on Marcia's. 'Tell me, my boy, how long—how long before we can all feel safe again?'

'Oh, it will be a day or two before they have the equipment ready, and then there'll be nothing to worry about. We'll wipe these things off the earth as if they'd never existed.

'In Russia of course it'll take time. A lot of time, but as far as this country is concerned we've got off very lightly.'

He said lightly, and it meant nothing, nothing at all. In the back of his mind was Roberts and the hours of agony, the *Gadshill* and the thing on the laboratory floor above, that would live for days till the counter-rays reached it, Mrs. Baker and the women of Durford. All the flotsam of the last five days. His hand reached across the table and took Marcia's.

'Well, my sweet, you'll be able to sleep at last, won't you? And you, General, have you tied up all your loose ends now?'

'More or less, my boy, more or less. There are still one or two points I'm not sure of. The spread of the stuff for instance, the spores I mean. How did she do it? It seems so fantastic that it should have got as far as Russia if it was merely the wind.'

Tony smiled a crooked smile at him. 'Oh no, General not the wind, it wasn't the wind ; she puts it here.' He leaned over and picked up the file again. 'Yes, it seems she wanted the first outbreak to take place in a remote area where it would not be noticed too soon and allowed to take root. The local attack was probably accidental. She used birds—'

'Birds! Sorry, I'm afraid I don't follow you.'

'Yes, it's quite simple really. Birds, migratory birds, swifts to be exact. Birds all bent on one thing, returning home for the summer. They couldn't be fully infected of course, but they could still be carriers. Not a very pleasant idea is it? Blue wings, blue wings on the water, wings taking something with them.'

'Thank you. Yes, as you say, not a nice thought.' Kirk blew his nose violently. 'Well, that's that. Only one thing more and I'm finished. I've got to know if she had any accomplices, apart from Roberts. Not likely, but I must be sure. That feller Loser for example. You're quite certain that she said nothing that suggested that?'

He watched them shake their heads, and stood up. 'Well, let's go then. I'll run you home. Don't bother about these papers, I'll see Hearn gets them very soon. They've rung him and he's standing by. Probably give the chap a knighthood after it's all over.'

He tightened his coat carefully, picked up the file, and opened the door. For the last time, they walked out through the dark hall, the incense, and the faded lithographs into the breaking light.

*

They asked Kirk to drop them at the end of the quad and walked slowly home across the grass. The sun was quite high now and the sky pale around the loom of the cathedral. They were almost to the house, their arms around each other, when Marcia stopped.

'Tony, that last question of Kirk's, about the accomplices, about whether she said anything.'

'But she didn't, did she, darling?' He was very tired. 'She didn't say a thing; she had no accomplices, only Roberts.'

'But she did say something, Tony. Don't you remember what she said, what she kept on saying, just before the—just before she died. It was the word "Lee", wasn't it, darling? Over and over again, she kept saying "Lee", and then "Many".'

She looked up at his face and saw understanding grow.

'Yes,' he said, and there was suddenly a great wonder in his voice. 'Yes, you're probably right. That's what she said, what he said. The man by the lake. The madman with a devil who ran about the tombs and they couldn't bind. "Lee." "My Name is Legion, for we are many." Yes, you're quite right she had accomplices.'

He looked at her, and then past her, up at the bulk of the

cathedral with its towers clear in the light and the rooks above and the hills behind. The dark, moorland hills that stretched away from it. Far away from it. Miles away from it. A long way away from it. A long way, a sad way, a cold way. All the way to the Solway. But not as far as the way that Rosa Steinberg had gone.

THE END